Calmly, Dav

'I'm not marrie
girlfriend or any prospect of either. I'm here to
concentrate on my work.'

He went on, 'Since we're going to get to know
each other, and work together, perhaps you
ought to tell me about yourself. I see no ring
on your finger. Are you married, engaged or,
as they say, do you have a partner?'

Jane was taken aback by this. But since she
had just asked him the same thing, she
supposed it was a fair question. 'No, I've
nobody at the moment. I'm footloose and
fancy-free.'

He fixed her with those amazing blue eyes.
'You surprise me,' he said quietly. 'I would
have thought a very attractive girl like yourself
would have been snapped up quickly.
But still...perhaps you're looking for the
right man.'

Gill Sanderson is a psychologist who finds time to write only by staying up late at night. Weekends are filled by her hobbies of gardening, running and mountain walking. Her ideas come from her work, from one son who is an oncologist, one son who is a nurse and her daughter who is a midwife. She first wrote articles for learned journals and chapters for a textbook. Then she was encouraged to change to fiction by her husband, who is an established writer of war stories.

Recent titles by the same author:

A MAN TO BE TRUSTED
A SON FOR JOHN
SEVENTH DAUGHTER

THE TIME IS NOW

BY
GILL SANDERSON

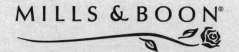

MILLS & BOON®

MILLS & BOON and MILLS & BOON with the Rose Device are registered trademarks of the publisher.

First published in Great Britain 2000
Harlequin Mills & Boon Limited,
Eton House, 18-24 Paradise Road, Richmond, Surrey TW9 1SR

© Gill Sanderson 2000

ISBN 0 263 82261 3

Set in Times Roman 10½ on 12 pt.
03-0009-51938

Printed and bound in Spain
by Litografia Rosés, S.A., Barcelona

CHAPTER ONE

'ALL you do is stand behind me and watch me,' Scrub Nurse Jane Cabot told Mary Barnes, the nervous student nurse standing next to her in Theatre. 'I'll try to tell you what I'm doing and why, but if I don't have time, remember to ask me afterwards.'

'There's a lot to remember,' Mary said, 'and it's my first time in Theatre. I hope I don't do anything wrong. I usually carry a notebook with me, which I can refer to.'

'It's a good idea. But not in an antiseptic environment.' Jane had seen the notebook in question when the two of them had scrubbed up. Of course, it had been left behind.

The nurses in Theatre were her responsibility, a responsibility she took very seriously. She looked critically at Mary, making sure that there were no wisps of dark hair showing. Mr Steadman—years ago, before they'd come to know each other better—had once shouted at her, asking her what the junior nurse was doing with spiders' legs sticking out from under her cap. Since then Jane had been careful about hair. Her own long blonde hair was held tight in a French plait, pinned safely on top of her head.

'You'll be all right,' she told Mary. 'Remember what you've been told, and try to relax. Don't get too tense.'

'This Mr Steadman. He's got the reputation of being a bit of a tartar.'

'He's a good surgeon—he just likes to have things

done right.' Jane smiled, even though she knew Mary couldn't see her lips. 'I had a new nurse in here once, just watching, like you, but she was so tense and breathing so heavily that she went into tetany.'

'Tetany?' It was obviously a new word for Mary.

'It's most commonly found in infants with too little ionic calcium in their blood, but adults can get it, too. The muscles go into spasm. The commonest feature is called Chvostek's sign, where the muscles of the face contract when the cheek is tapped. Anyway, I sent her out and she took some calcitrol, and the next time she came in she was fine. So don't breathe too heavily.'

Mary reached backwards, seeking her notebook. But it wasn't there. 'Will you run through that with me afterwards, please?' she asked.

'Happy to. Now relax.'

In fact, the little lecture Jane had just given had had the desired effect. Mary now had something to think about, to remember, and her body grew noticeably less rigid. 'Just do what I tell you, and never move too quickly. You'll be all right. You're here to learn.'

'Morning, Jane, Dr Lane.' Mr Steadman swept into the theatre, followed by two students. He nodded at the anaesthetist. The surgeon was a short, broad-shouldered man, aged about fifty-five, with terrifying eyebrows above his green mask. 'Now, first of all we have an abdominal hysterectomy. Reason—uterine fibroids.'

Without looking up, Mr Steadman reached out his hand and Jane placed in it the scalpel she knew he'd need. The first incision. She reached for the diathermy machine to seal off the blood vessels. The operation proceeded. The surgeon was skilful, fast—everything and everyone was working well.

The mishap was only a minor one. Jane had moved

away from her trolley to fetch more swabs, but Mr Steadman was in a hurry. 'Retractor! Retractor!' he bellowed.

Mary blinked—perhaps he was shouting at her? She reached, confused, towards the trolley.

'Get your hands off those instruments!' This was more than a bellow.

Jane returned swiftly to her place and handed the required instrument to the surgeon. 'Retractor, Mr Steadman.'

There was a grunt, and the operation proceeded. Jane looked at the quivering nurse by her side and winked at her.

Later there was a more serious delay on another case. It wasn't a major operation, being the excision of a blocked Bartholin cyst. But where was the patient? Apparently there was a problem with the anaesthetic and the anaesthetist wasn't quite ready. Mr Steadman stood, silent with rage. Eventually the patient was wheeled in, the anaesthetist behind him.

'Sorry, got caught up in something,' the anaesthetist said eventually.

'It was good of you to join us,' Mr Steadman said. 'May I begin now?'

'Edmund, this is Nurse Mary Barnes. She's trying to learn. Today was her first day ever in Theatre and you were unkind to her.'

The morning's list was finished. Jane was in the anteroom with her student nurse, and Mr Steadman was walking through. The surgeon looked at the flinching Mary and then at Jane, who stared serenely back at him. After a pause he said, 'I remember my first day in Theatre. Can be a bit of a shock. Just do what Cabot here tells you, and in time you might be as good a scrub nurse as she is.'

Then he turned and left, and Jane heard Mary sigh with relief. 'See, he is human,' Jane said. 'Now, come on and we'll get out of these greens. Then you report back to the ward.'

'How come you can speak to the old man like that? I daren't.'

Jane was in the corridor, walking towards the hospital canteen, when Henry Lane, the anaesthetist, fell in beside her. She looked at him, a middle-aged, rotund little man with a permanent scowl on his face.

'We've been together for a long time.' She shrugged. 'He forgives me a lot.'

'More than he forgives anyone else. Well, I'm leaving soon and, quite frankly, I'll be glad. That little oversight of mine in the theatre—any competent surgeon could have dealt with it.'

She wasn't having that. Edmund Steadman could be awkward, but he was her friend and, more than that, he was completely, ruthlessly professional.

'I would have said that any competent anaesthetist would have ensured that the situation didn't arise in the first place.'

Henry Lane stopped short and looked at her furiously. 'You're only a nurse! Are you questioning my professional—?'

'Yes, as a matter of fact, I am,' Jane said briskly. 'I think Mr Steadman was absolutely right.' She wasn't going to be browbeaten by this man. 'And, incidentally, I am not "only a nurse"—I am a nurse and a good one. We all have our jobs in Theatre, and we rely on each other.'

For a moment the two glared at each other and then

the anaesthetist obviously decided not to carry on the conversation. He muttered something inaudible and walked away. Jane was glad—if he argued she was going to argue back. You got nowhere in this world if you didn't stand up for what you knew was right.

There were none of her particular friends in the canteen so she sat by herself to eat her salad. However, five minutes later Edmund Steadman walked in, collected a steaming plate of the day's special—roast beef, potatoes and Yorkshire pudding—and came over to join her.

'Calories, Edmund!' Jane said, pointing with her fork.

'I need the energy, and so do you. We're working all afternoon.'

Edmund could have eaten his lunch in the consultants' dining room, but always preferred to eat in the main canteen. Once he'd told her, half-jokingly, that the canteen was the hospital's brain, not its stomach. 'Everything important is discussed here, Jane. You'd be surprised what I've picked up.'

Now he said, 'Have you heard that Lane is leaving soon? I'll be glad to get rid of him. The man's a menace.'

'Hush, Edmund! Let's have a bit of professionalism! You're not supposed to complain about other doctors to the nursing staff.'

'Professionalism is no excuse for idleness or incompetence. But I suppose you're right.' He tasted his beef with obvious enjoyment. 'I still miss Judy.'

'So do I. I phoned her last night. She sends her love and says everything is going well.'

Judy Parsons had been the anaesthetist Edmund had always used. The three of them had formed a team that could almost reach each other's minds. But Judy had left to have her first baby, and had told the team quite firmly that there was no chance of her returning for at least a year. 'It's too risky a job when your mind is on other things, and your body is tired, too. You won't see me until I'm certain I'm ready.'

'So who is replacing Dr Lane?'

'We're appointing a new consultant anaesthetist. Picked a young fellow from Lady Mary Hospital in Birmingham—he's very well recommended. Name's David Kershaw. He would have come earlier so we didn't have to put up with rubbish like Lane, but they wanted to hang onto him. He'd better fit in.'

'I'm sure he will,' Jane said, deciding to say nothing about Edmund's loud remarks about their present anaesthetist. 'Now, we've got an interesting case this afternoon...'.

It had been a good but tiring day. She changed into her trousers and the jacket with the fluorescent patches and trotted across the quadrangle to the boiler-house where she left her bicycle under the watchful eye of her friend, Herbert, the boilerman. Whenever the weather permitted it, she left her car at home. After a hard day in Theatre she enjoyed the exercise, cycling the five miles to Challis.

Her hospital was Emmy's—the Emmeline Penistone Women's Hospital. It was in an area which once had been the home of rich middle-class merchants. Now most of the ornate Victorian terraced houses had been converted and subdivided. It was an area for students and for transients. Cars regularly disappeared from outside Emmy's—and bikes, too, even when securely fastened to railings. So Jane left her bike inside the boiler-house.

She shouted a greeting to Herbert, collected her bike and fastened on her scarlet helmet. Once she had scrubbed for an operation on a fourteen-year-old cyclist who'd had a depressed fracture of the skull. 'If every cyclist wore a helmet,' the surgeon had said, 'then I should be out of work.'

It was October now, and getting chillier as she cycled home. But she would cycle as long as she could. The five miles passed quickly, and she now knew all the short cuts.

She shared a house in Challis with two other girls— Sue, a midwife, and Megan, a senior house officer. They had been together for two years, now all working in the same hospital. They got on well because they didn't live in each other's pockets, but this evening she knew that things might be a little different.

She unlocked the front door, and smiled. Bobbing against the ceiling, there was a collection of brightly coloured, helium-filled balloons, with streamers dangling from them. The biggest balloon, a purple one, had a message on it—HAPPY 29TH BIRTHDAY, JANE! Sue and Megan heard her come in and rushed out of the kitchen to kiss her.

'You're not allowed in the kitchen, birthday girl,' Sue said. 'Into the front room and have a drink until the meal is ready.'

'It practically is ready,' said Megan. 'Let's all have a drink. And a parcel came for you this morning, Jane, from London.'

Jane sat, and accepted a glass of chilled white wine, poured with due solemnity. None of the three drank to any great extent. Then she smiled as she opened her small parcel, for she recognised the handwriting on the outside. Inside were three CDs, chosen with care, and a birthday card, reading, 'Happy Birthday, Sister'. Someone had inserted the word 'scrub' before 'sister'. Inside was a message. 'Much love, big sister. I'm working like mad, enjoying every minute of it—though there's plenty to do and learn. With any luck I'll get a couple of days soon and come up to see you. Big-headed me is sending you a picture. Love again! Peter.

It was a good picture, of a curly-haired lad in a regulation white coat, smiling outside a gloomy London hospital.

'Let's see,' said Sue. Jane passed it round and explained to Megan, 'It's my brother, Peter. You know he qualified as a doctor this summer, and this is his first house job.'

'He looks lovely. I envy you, Jane. I've got no brothers or sisters.'

'I have,' said Sue. 'Well, I suppose I have. And he's trouble. Anyway, here are our presents.'

From Megan Jane had a fine woollen scarf to keep her warm while she was cycling. From Sue there was a black silk teddy. Laughing, she stood, wrapped the scarf round her neck and held the teddy in front of her.

'Both suit you,' Megan said. 'That teddy looks very sexy.'

'The trouble is, no one is likely to see the teddy but me. No man, certainly. And it's a pity to keep it just for myself.'

'Give it time,' Sue advised. 'You're sure to find the right man. Now, let's go into the kitchen and eat. It should be ready by now, judging by the smell.'

The three were friends, but had decided early on that trying to eat together every day was too difficult. They all worked shifts, and had different obligations. So they had joint meals only occasionally, and when they did they enjoyed them the more. This evening's was a typical meal. Sue had cooked a hearty chicken curry with basmati rice, while Megan had created a number of dainty sambals. They had another glass of white wine each. All of them ate well—they worked hard and needed the energy.

Then, after much giggling in the pantry, Sue emerged with a cake, twenty-nine lit candles flickering on top. 'Shut your eyes, blow and wish,' she said, after the cake had been carefully deposited on the table. 'But don't burn your eyebrows.'

Jane took a great breath, shut her eyes and blew. The other two cheered.

'I'm not having any more birthdays,' Jane said as Sue efficiently cut the cake. 'You won't be able to find a cake big enough to hold all the candles.'

'Rubbish,' Sue said, passing her an inordinately large slice. 'You're still only a child. Now, Megan's filled the glasses so here's to you, Jane!'

'It's the big three-O next time,' Jane said gloomily. 'My biological clock is ticking. This year is my last chance. Either I find a man or I give up and become a medical old maid. I'll put the fear of God into all the new young doctors and nurses.'

'You do that already,' Megan put in, 'you and that Mr Steadman.'

'He's a good surgeon,' Jane said amiably. 'He just wants everything to work perfectly. Not much to ask, is it?'

'Anyway, what's wrong with the men you meet already?' Sue chipped in. 'You've got dozens of male friends. What about Eric Thingy? You know, the radiographer fellow. I saw you with him a lot in the canteen.'

'Not any more,' Jane said darkly. 'That's well over. All he wanted was a sock-washing woman. He asked me if I'd like to move in with him. Invited me round to his flat. I took one look at it and decided that the bachelor life had gone on too long. There was no way I was going to try to civilise *him*!'

The others laughed, and Megan said, 'Well, there was that solicitor you went out with last year. The one with the big black car.'

'Reggie? Could you really imagine being married to a man called Reggie? I never found out, but I suspect that even his pyjamas were pinstriped. He wanted a *respectable* wife. No, I'm happy in my job, and I've seen so many people take second best and then be miserable that I'm not going to do it myself. It's the right man or none at all. And at present it looks like none at all. Now, it's my birthday and I fancy another piece of cake. And how about—?'

The telephone rang. There were extensions throughout the house, one very useful one in the kitchen. Jane picked up the receiver, and a female voice said, 'Jane?' When she answered in the affirmative she heard a loud rendition of 'Happy Birthday to You', then a giggle and the questions, 'Guess who? And how's the birthday girl?'

'Hi, Ann,' said Jane cheerfully. 'I'm doing fine. Even after a year, who could forget that singing voice?' Ann Deeds was an old friend, a nurse she'd trained with who'd left the hospital for promotion down south just over a year before. 'How are things with you?'

'I guess I'm much the same as ever. Getting older, like we all are.' Jane thought she caught a touch of desolation in her friend's voice. Ann went on, 'I was just thinking of last year's party, of you doing your impression of Marlene Dietrich, and I had to phone. Going to do that impression tonight?'

'I think I'm getting a bit old for making a fool of myself like that.'

'Nonsense! Last year you sang "Falling in Love Again" and kissed that American doctor who was sitting at the bar. He fell off his stool.'

'I remember! He'd had too much to drink and thought I meant it. Then he spent the next six weeks chasing me round the wards.'

Ann giggled again. 'If you go to the club tonight, I'll bet they persuade you. I'm sorry I won't be there.'

'So am I. We…' Something suddenly struck Jane. 'Just a minute! You're at Lady Mary Hospital. We're getting an anaesthetist from you. David…Earnshaw?'

'David Kershaw,' Ann said, too quickly. 'Yes, I believe you are.'

Jane detected the inflection Ann was trying to hide. 'So you know him. What's he like?'

'He's a very good doctor. You'll have no trouble from him…professionally. He's keen, conscientious, interested. The surgeons here are very sorry to lose him.'

Jane thought for a moment, then went on, 'The way you said that means you're not telling me something. Come on, Ann, let's hear the worst.'

'He's stunning,' said Ann, 'absolutely gorgeous. He looks like a Greek god, he really does. I think he's the most beautiful man I've ever met in my life.'

'Is he married, and if not why not?'

'No, he's not married. He says he doesn't want to be. He's only interested in a casual relationship—he's very up front about it. Tells you right from the start.'

'So that's what he told *you* right from the start?'

'I guess so.' Ann sighed. 'And I'm not the only one.'

'He sounds a real louse.'

'No, he's not! He was fair. He told me not to…not to get too fond of him, but I did. If I got into trouble then it was entirely my own fault.'

'I'll bet it was. I've heard this "I only want a casual relationship" thing before. Now, tell me about work…'

They exchanged a few other details and then rang off.

'That was Ann Deeds. How is she doing?' Sue asked. She had worked with Ann before.

'Seems to be all right,' Jane said thoughtfully. 'We're getting a new anaesthetist, and Ann has worked with him. Apparently he's a bit of a lady-killer.'

'You'll cope,' Megan said. 'You always do. Lord help the lady-killer who tries anything on with you.'

Jane shook her head. 'Coping isn't enough. In Theatre you have to work as a team, know each other's feelings so nothing need be said. When we had Judy Parsons we were a real team, but this latest fellow Lane has been a disaster. Mr Steadman really dislikes him, and he's entitled to. I just want someone who can fit in.'

'Like I said, you'll cope. Come on, the party's over now—let's clear away.'

The one golden rule in their shared house was that everything had to be washed and cleared away at once. Sue was working later. Jane was going out and for once had managed to persuade Megan to come with her. Megan seldom went out.

Party time! Jane undid her French plait and shook it out. People at work who had only ever seen her with her hair up were sometimes amazed to see that when loose it was waist-length. She had a shower, combed out her hair, blow-dried it and fastened it back with two tortoiseshell clips. Then she put on a white T-shirt and a dark red floaty skirt split up to the thigh. If she was going to dance, she wanted to feel untrammelled. A quick touch of make-up, a look at herself in the mirror and she had to admit that she didn't look bad.

'You look wonderful,' Megan said when she got downstairs. 'You look as if you're going to enjoy yourself.'

'I *am* going to enjoy myself,' Jane said with resolution.

They took a taxi together to the clubhouse on the outskirts of town where Jane played hockey for the university. It was an ancient, rickety, wooden building, but she'd had some good times there. Nearly every Saturday she played on the pitch nearby if no emergency work had come up, and there was always a bit of a party after the match. She'd arranged to be picked up by taxi as this was mid-week and she knew that most people wouldn't want to stay too late.

Holding the hesitant Megan firmly by the hand, she entered the building. The little bar was decked with streamers—the same ones came out for Christmas and any other function. But the place looked cheerful. There was music already, and a couple were circling the tiny dance-floor. They had a resident DJ, an electronics student who was the only person who dared to touch the antiquated equipment.

Technically Jane had hired the clubhouse, though it hadn't cost her much. She'd ordered sausage rolls, sandwiches and so on from the catering manager, and had invited friends from the hospital and the hockey team. Basically this was just an excuse to see friends and dance.

There was a great cheer as she walked in, and everyone sang 'Happy Birthday to You'. She was kissed by more men—and women—than she could count. She accepted the first drink she was offered, and after that resolutely refused all further alcohol. It was an amiable, noisy party, just the sort she enjoyed. She danced, she talked, she laughed. It was a good night.

After a while a few newcomers came to her party, mostly hospital people who'd just finished a shift. She was surprised to see Edmund Steadman among them. She had invited him, of course, but hadn't expected him to turn up. He was dressed casually in a black shirt over blue jeans. Another surprise—she'd never seen him out of formal clothes before.

'Edmund, it's so lovely of you to come! Let me get you a drink.'

'Let me get you one. You're the birthday girl.'

'I've had plenty already, Edmund,' she whispered. 'You know me, nothing to excess. But you can dance with me if you like.'

'I would like that indeed.'

'And now we're playing a golden oldie,' boomed the DJ at that moment. 'Partly in recognition of the vast age of our beloved Jane, partly because all we have left are Beatles numbers. Ladies and gentlemen, ''Love me Do''.'

To her amazement, Edmund Steadman was an excellent dancer. He whirled her round so that her skirt billowed round her waist, then caught her, lifted her off her feet, steered her in the most complex of moves. He was marvellous!

'Edmund, you're a fantastic dancer!' she said breathlessly as they walked back to the bar. 'Where did you learn to move like that?'

'Even I was young once,' he said solemnly, 'and, as

I calculate, it was in the sixties. Now, I have a present for you.' He took out a small wooden box, with oriental script on the outside. 'You remember I did a tour of the Far East a few months ago—Singapore, Hong Kong and so on—a bit of lecturing, a few operations. Well, I brought back a few trinkets. I'd like you to have this. And before you say anything, Marion knows I'm giving it to you, and she thoroughly approves and sends her best wishes. She would have liked to come, but you know…'

Jane had met Marion several times before and the two women got on well. Marion Steadman was quiet and retiring, just the opposite of her ebullient husband. Unfortunately, she suffered from severe arthritis, for which there was no suitable treatment.

Jane opened the box. Inside was a silver chain with a jade pendant in the form of an intricately carved dragon. 'Edmund, this is beautiful!'

'I'm glad you like it. You're the best scrub nurse I've ever had, Jane. I'm glad you're on my team. Now, one more dance and then I'll leave you young people.'

It was still a good night. She danced with everyone, chatted, laughed. Later on someone brought out a top hat from its hiding place behind the bar and found her a hockey stick. For a while the disco was silent, and someone sat behind the old piano and played the introductory bars to 'Falling in Love Again'. She found herself being lifted bodily onto the bar, and once again had to strut along the top, doing her smoky Marlene Dietrich impression. It went down well.

The party eventually wound down. She kissed everyone else again, and was told her taxi was waiting outside. She left with Megan.

'You're a super singer,' said Megan. 'I bet you could do it professionally.'

'Well, I'm in the hospital choir, but I'd rather be a scrub nurse than a singer. Did you have a good time?'

'Yes, I did. I danced a bit, talked with one or two people. You really seemed to enjoy yourself. Mind you, you always do.'

'It was my birthday,' Jane said. In the darkness she closed her eyes. She always did enjoy herself. But next year—her thirtieth birthday—she thought she might like to have a change. But what sort of change?

'Good night last night,' Megan said next morning. 'I enjoyed myself.' She sat opposite Jane, the two of them in dressing-gowns, eating bowls of muesli. 'What's it feel like to be twenty-nine?'

'Very similar to being twenty-eight. Next year will be the telling birthday. Shall I make more tea?'

After she had filled the kettle she heard the bang of the letter-box and the smack of letters hitting the floor, so she went to fetch their mail.

All three girls got plenty of letters, among which was always a lot of junk medical mail. Jane sorted through the pile, pushing Megan's letters over to her and stacking Sue's on the corner of the table. Apart from the usual rubbish, she herself had a couple of belated birthday cards. She opened them and placed them with all the others on the cupboard in the corner. There was one envelope left, thick and official-looking. For some reason it made her feel uneasy.

'Me first in the bathroom,' Megan said. 'Take your time over your cup of tea.' And she was gone.

Alone now, Jane picked up the thick envelope, and turned it over a couple times. Then she ripped it open.

Inside was a sheet of paper and another sealed envelope. She looked at the sheet of paper, which was headed with the name of an agency. Twice she read the few, type-written paragraphs, and her face paled. She picked up the sealed envelope and shook it as if there might be something inside. Then she thrust envelope and sheet back inside the larger envelope.

Megan was still in the bathroom so no one had seen Jane's reaction. No one here knew the letter existed. Jane rushed upstairs, pulled open her stocking drawer and thrust the envelope at the back. She knew it wasn't like her. Jane prided herself that she faced all problems head on. Whatever life offered, she could take it. But she couldn't take this, not just yet. She had to have time. She'd open the letter when she was ready.

CHAPTER TWO

'DAVID, this is Jane Cabot, the best scrub nurse in the north of England. Jane, I'd like you to meet Dr David Kershaw, our new anaesthetist.'

It was the following Monday morning, and Jane was scrubbing up for the day's list. She turned to the two green-clad figures behind her, and the new anaesthetist held out his hand to her. 'Pleased to meet you, Jane. I hope we'll work well together.'

Her friend Ann had warned her, but the sight of him was still a shock. This new man was all that she'd said—and more. He was the most handsome—no, beautiful—man that Jane had ever seen. Even his voice was beautiful, soft and soothing. Almost an anaesthetic in itself, she found herself thinking wildly.

Speechless, she took the extended hand.

David Kershaw was tall. He towered over Edmund, and made even her own very respectable five feet nine inches seem petite. Shapeless greens hid his body, but she had the impression of broad shoulders and a slim waist. His head was covered with those golden curls traditionally given to Greek gods. Unusually, for a fair man, he had a slight tan. His eyes were the darkest blue possible and wonderfully curved lips covered the whitest of teeth.

This man is going to cause havoc among the younger nurses, she thought gloomily to herself. Then she realised that she'd said nothing yet, and recovered quickly. She was too old to be impressed by a pretty face.

'Welcome to Emmy's, Dr Kershaw,' she said. 'I hope you'll be happy here. It's a good place to work.'

'I've been made very welcome so far, and I'm looking forward to working here. But, please, call me David. Round the operating table everyone has a job to do and is equally important.' He glanced at Edmund, and added, straight-faced, 'Except for the surgeon, of course, who is most important.'

Edmund laughed and so did Jane. Good, the new anaesthetist had a sense of humour. At times in Theatre it was invaluable, if not taken too far. If things weren't going well with an operation, the entire Theatre could get tense. An atmosphere developed in which mistakes could be made. Edmund was a brilliant surgeon, but he was no good at defusing an atmosphere. Judy Parsons had been good at it, and with luck this man would be good, too.

The operating assistant poked his head cautiously round the corner of the door. 'Mr Steadman? We've got a bit of a problem with this form. If you've got a minute to sort it out…'

'Problem with a form!' stormed Edmund. 'I'm supposed to be a surgeon, not a clerk. I've got a…'

He saw Jane shaking her head at him, and sighed. 'All right, I'll come and see if I can sort it out. I'll be back in five minutes, you two. Just don't start without me.'

The door banged shut and Jane was alone with David Kershaw. There was a slight change in the atmosphere, and she thought that somehow things felt different. She wondered if he felt the same way, but she couldn't tell. It was strange. He hadn't said anything to her, and yet things were definitely…different. She found herself warming to him as she looked at him. And then she remembered the desolation in her friend Ann's voice, and decided to tease him a little.

'Are you married, David? If you have a wife we'd like to make her welcome. The hospital has quite a wide social life, and we'd like to introduce her to it. It must be strange, coming to a completely new town.'

Calmly, he shook his head. 'I'm not married, I don't have a partner, a girlfriend or any prospect of either. I'm here to concentrate on my work.'

He had an odd nervous gesture, she noticed. His body remained perfectly still, very relaxed, but he rubbed the inside of the fingers of his right hand with the fingertips of his left. It was a gentle, caressing movement.

He went on, 'Since we're going to get to know each other, and work together, perhaps you ought to tell me about yourself. I see no ring on your finger. Are you married, engaged or, as they say, do you have a partner?'

She was taken aback by this. But since she had just asked him the same thing, she supposed it was a fair question. 'No, I've nobody at the moment. I'm foot-loose and fancy-free.'

He fixed her with those amazing blue eyes. 'You surprise me,' he said quietly. 'I would have thought a very attractive girl like yourself would have been snapped up quickly. But still…perhaps you're looking for the right man.'

She realised that calling her a very attractive girl wasn't a come-on, but a simple statement of fact. She rather liked it. And, she had to admit, she was flattered, too. But it was definitely time to change the subject. Things were getting a little too personal.

'Where are you living?' she asked.

She was answered in the same calm tones. 'For the

moment I have a place in the hospital. But I put down a deposit for a flat on Ransome's Wharf yesterday. I hope to move in in a week or two.'

She blinked. She knew of Ransome's Wharf. It was a set of converted warehouses overlooking the river. The conversions had been expensive, and the view of the Welsh hills beyond the river made them even more desirable. 'That's nice,' she said. 'I'm sure you'll be comfortable there.'

'I've lived in furnished places for too long. I want to put down roots now.'

His voice was so calm, so musical, that she felt it lulling her. It gave her confidence in the man, as if he— She jerked her thoughts back to normal.

'You've got a very musical voice,' she said boldly. 'Do you sing at all?'

'Only in the bath. And then quite quietly.'

'I'm in the hospital choir. We're always looking for new voices, especially male voices. Why don't you come for an audition?'

He shook his head, obviously amused. 'First of all, I have to settle down in the job. Secondly, I've never sung to anyone but myself, and I don't fancy the idea of being in a choir. We have to be a team in Theatre, and I like that. But outside work—socially—I tend to be a bit of a loner.'

'You don't like company?'

'Yes, I do. But I like it on my own terms. I'm not very keen on the compulsory enjoyment of parties. A small group of two, three or four is my idea of a good time.'

Jane remembered the numbers at her own party last week, how much she had enjoyed seeing everyone, and winced. She didn't really have a lot in common with this man, did she?

Before she could answer, Edmund was back in the room. 'Problem sorted,' he said. 'David, the first case is on her way up. D'you want to go and do your bit?'

'I'll see you in Theatre,' David said. 'You, too, Jane.'

It had sounded almost like an invitation. An intimate invitation.

However, she had her own work to do. She went to scrub up, side by side with the trainee Mary Barnes again, who was coming along well. As she scrubbed she thought about David Kershaw. Yes, he was beautiful. But she'd liked him. She'd met very handsome men before, who were well aware of their own good looks and the effect they had on women. She felt that David was aware of the effect he had, but that he wouldn't delight in it or trade on it. She liked him for that. Then she remembered. He'd hurt her friend, even though Ann didn't hold it against him. Perhaps he was much more cunning than she'd given him credit for.

Usually the anaesthetist sat by the patient's head, keeping a keen eye on his own concerns and only looking occasionally at the work of the surgeon. But she noticed that although David was obviously competent at his own job he appeared fascinated by what Edmund was doing, and even on occasion peered over to have a closer look. Edmund found this interesting, and explained what he was doing to David as well as his two students. Jane found it curious, too.

It was the end of another good, hard day and, as ever, she'd enjoyed herself. As she wheeled her bike out of the boiler-house she decided she was going to enjoy working with David Kershaw. Already she could feel herself slipping into a partnership in which she, Edmund and David worked together. And David and Edmund seemed to like and respect each other. That was important. Edmund and Dr Lane had never got on. Yes, she could work with David. And she didn't need to worry about his private life, did she?

Behind her she heard the growl of an engine, something much more powerful than was usually heard in the hospital car park. She turned as a silver sports car drew up alongside her. David looked out of the window.

He'd changed into civvies—a black leather jacket and a white open-necked shirt. In front of him she could see an array of dials on a rather frightening dashboard. He looked as if he fitted in the car, was perfectly at home.

'You make me feel ashamed of myself,' he said in his calm voice. 'Every now and again I give talks to women's clubs about the respiratory system, the dangers of smoking, the value of exercise. Now I see you on a health-giving bicycle and I'm in this silver monster.'

'I know it's a Porsche,' she told him. 'Apparently the engineering is wonderful. My little brother says he wants one when he can afford it.'

'Your little brother? Scrub Nurse Cabot, do you realise you're making me feel like a perpetual adolescent? Still, if your brother approves, you might. Would you like a ride in it some time? I could take you into the surrounding countryside and you could show me around a bit. Perhaps we could have a drink or something.'

She looked at him in amazement. 'You don't waste much time, do you? You only got here today.'

He shrugged. 'I'm a stranger here, I know no one socially. We're going to be colleagues and probably friends. I certainly hope so. It's just that I'd like to talk to you out of the hospital atmosphere. And I already know that you're not attached at the moment.'

The invitation was utterly unexpected and her first reaction was to refuse at once. She wondered why. She knew she was capable of looking after herself.

'All right,' she said. 'I'd like a ride in your silver car so I can make my little brother jealous.'

She looked at his face intently. If he showed the slightest hint of masculine self-satisfaction, if his face betrayed the slightest hint that he thought he'd made a conquest, she'd change her mind at once. She'd seen the expression on faces of other men who'd thought they were God's gift to women.

But not this one. He just looked quietly pleased. 'Good,' he said. 'When can we arrange it?'

She thought ahead, knowing there was some flexibility in her hours. 'Could you manage late Wednesday afternoon?' she asked. 'That is, if nothing comes up.'

'Wednesday afternoon will suit me fine—I think I can organise my timetable. But this is a hospital and I know something can always come up.' He smiled at her. 'Looking forward to it no end, Jane. We'll sort out the details on Wednesday morning.' He raised his hand, the engine purred more loudly and the car drew away. She noticed that he stuck rigidly to the speed limit the hospital tried—often in vain—to enforce.

She felt herself warming to him, pleased that he'd said he was looking forward to being with her. Only when she started cycling home did she wonder how many other women had fallen for that same smile. One thing was certain. She wasn't going to.

For some reason she cycled back more energetically than usual. Once home she found that Sue was equally warm through working in the garden, and the two sat in the kitchen and had a coffee.

'How's the new anaesthetist?' Sue asked, pushing

over a packet of chocolate biscuits. 'Is he as gorgeous as Ann said?'

'He's good, very competent. Most important, he's going to get on with Edmund Steadman. He is as gorgeous as Ann said and he's taking me out on Wednesday afternoon.'

Sue looked dubious. 'Are you sure that's a good idea? He's moving a bit quickly.'

'It's probably not a good idea,' Jane said cheerfully. 'But I'm a big girl, I've been forewarned and I can look after myself. Our friendship will be casual—on my terms.'

Sue smiled. 'Something tells me the wonderful Dr David Kershaw might have met his match.'

But Jane wasn't so sure.

Both of them managed to get the time off on Wednesday. 'Pick me up at my house,' she told him that morning. 'The hospital will gossip in time but we don't have to make it easy for them.'

'That suits me fine. I don't like being gossiped about.'

I'll bet you don't, she thought to herself, but said nothing.

She cycled home at lunchtime, and then irritated herself by thinking too hard about what she should wear. After all, they were only colleagues going out for a friendly drink. Still, she wanted to look, well, attractive. She took out the teddy Sue had given her, then put it back. Definitely not.

The Porsche was a low-slung sports car so, bearing in mind the difficulty of getting in and out, she decided to wear a pair of black velvet trousers. With them she wore a simple black sweater, and put to hand the navy blue fleece she wore to the sports ground. She unpinned her hair, shook it out and brushed it. Then she waited, telling herself that she wasn't impatient.

When he rang the doorbell late in the afternoon she tried to force herself not to rush to the front door. Then she decided that was childish, and ran as she usually did. He was wearing the black leather jacket again, but this time with a dark blue shirt and trousers. He looked wonderful, the darkness of his clothes contrasting with the gold of his hair.

In his turn, he was shocked. 'Your hair, I didn't realise it was so long,' he said. 'It's really beautiful.'

It was a short but obviously sincere compliment. 'My sole vice,' she told him. 'I know it's impractical in Theatre so I keep it pinned up. But I've always had long hair and I like it. When I unpin it, it makes me feel free.' She shook her head so that her hair billowed round her.

He reached out to catch a strand. 'It's like spun gold,' he said.

'Look at us two. Both dressed in black and both with yellow hair. People will take us for brother and sister.'

'Oh, I do hope not,' he said.

They walked down to the car, where he opened the door for her to get in then climbed in himself. The methodical fastening of seat belts followed. She'd never been in a car like this before and found it rather exciting. They weren't sitting but semi-reclining. The black leather seats were surprisingly comfortable, and in front of her was a bewildering selection of dials and levers—very different from her own six-year-old Fiesta. Even the subdued roar of the engine sounded expensive.

Earlier in the day, when they'd finalised their arrangements, they'd decided to go to the Black Lion, a pub in Wales she'd visited before. She'd told him that she didn't want dinner because she'd have to be back quite early—just a sandwich or something would do.

'I hope we can do a little better than that.'

'Well, the Black Lion has pizza ovens, and the pizzas are supposed to be very good.'

So the Black Lion had been decided on. Now she asked, 'Do you want directions? We turn left onto the main road and then—'

'Not necessary. I looked up the place on the map and memorised the route. You just lie back and enjoy the ride. Now…this is what a Porsche can do.'

They had threaded their way through the suburbs onto the slip-road for the motorway. He put his foot down on the curve, and as the car accelerated for the first time she understood the thrill that speed brought. The contoured seat held her as her neck and back were forced backwards. The engine was snarling now and she laughed with sheer exhilaration. 'Different from your Ford Fiesta?' he asked.

'Just a bit!'

David was a good driver and drove the car fast but well, taking no stupid risks. 'When I'm driving fast I tend not to talk,' he told her. 'I can only do one thing well at once so pick a tape if you like.' He indicated a full rack.

She didn't pick a tape. Instead, she pushed the appropriate button to see what was already in the deck. To her great surprise she heard a Gregorian chant. 'I didn't expect this of you,' she said.

He grinned. 'What did you expect, then?'

'Something like Sinatra's *Songs for Swinging Lovers*?'

'I think I'd better concentrate on my driving,' he said. 'I'll answer that remark later.'

For half an hour they drove, Jane telling him which places were interesting to visit, along with a bit of history. It was getting dark by the time they reached their turn-off to the maze of little roads that led to the Black Lion. 'I could map-read now if you want,' she offered.

Once again he shook his head. 'Still no need. I had a good look at the map—it'll be a bit of a test to see if I can remember the route.'

And he did get it right. They drove up to the Black Lion, which was an old whitewashed pub, with an il-luminated car park. She had been there before, and David liked the place at once. 'One of the troubles with Birmingham is that it's too hard to get out of,' he said. 'This is in the country, and it's great.'

They found an alcove to sit in and ordered a pizza each, choosing from a bewildering variety of toppings. The pizzas would take about twenty minutes, they were told. Jane asked for a glass of white wine and David for a glass of red. 'Top limit is two glasses when I'm driving,' he said. 'I'm a bit particular about drinking and driving.'

'I'm very pleased to hear that.'

The drinks were placed on the table in front of them, but neither of them made a move to pick theirs up. Instead, they looked at each other speculatively. Then she smiled, perhaps a little too sweetly.

'Now you're going to warn me,' she said. 'You're going to tell me that you're only interested in a casual relationship and I'm not to take you seriously. Anything between us will just be a fun thing. There is absolutely no prospect of any long-term commitment—anything like marriage, for example. But we can still have a good time together.'

He blinked, lifted his glass to his mouth, sipped from it and then coughed and spluttered. He groped in his pocket for a handkerchief. 'I think that's the most offputting thing any woman has ever said to me,' he said eventually. 'What on earth made you say it?'

'Just tell me that you weren't going to say something like that—if not now, then in the next couple of times we were out—and I'll apologise.'

He was shrewd, she already knew that. 'You've been checking up on me.'

'Not exactly. I heard about you purely by accident. I've got a very good friend who works at Lady Mary Hospital in Birmingham. Ann Deeds. Remember her?'

'Yes, I remember her very well. But I thought we parted good friends.'

'You did part good friends. She still likes you. She says that you warned her, said that the affair was casual, that you couldn't have been more honest.'

'So why are you holding it against me?'

She looked at him, wide-eyed. 'I'm not holding anything against you. How could I? I've come out with you. I'm enjoying your company. I even gave your little speech about a casual relationship to save you the trouble. However, I would suggest that saying a relationship must remain casual is a bit of a cop-out. You ought to know that, in spite of you saying that, a lot of women will still take you seriously.'

'Yes, I'd thought of that. And each time I'm sorry. But I like the company of women. Jane, I don't think you're being really fair to me.'

'I hope you're not going to say that it's not your fault that they suffer,' she threatened.

'No. I know it's my fault.' He seemed to have recovered a little from his initial shock as he sipped more wine and looked at her curiously. 'This is unusual. I feel I have to justify myself to you. It's not something I'm accustomed to feeling.'

'I hope you're not going to quote *My Fair Lady* to me, and ask why a woman can't be more like a man. Because the answer is simple. They're different.'

'So I see. Jane, I'm sorry I'm not the man you thought I was. We'll have our pizzas and then I'll take you back home.'

She looked at him in surprise. 'Why? We're enjoying each other's company. What you want I want, too. Just to sit here and talk.'

'Yes, but…'

Their pizzas arrived. They were on wooden plates, already cut into slices, and their smell was truly wonderful.

'Saved by the pizza,' he said. 'This smells too good to argue over. Can we have a truce while we eat?'

'Truce,' she agreed. 'Aren't anchovies super?'

After they'd finished their pizzas they both agreed that, though they didn't really need it, they would have ice cream, too. That was also wonderful. To finish they ordered espresso coffees, then smiled contentedly at each other and agreed that it was a bit odd to have such successful Italian food in a rural Welsh pub.

'I guess I was a bit ratty with you earlier,' she said. 'Perhaps my blood sugar was low—I've had nothing to eat since my muesli breakfast.'

'More bad decisions are taken through low blood sugar than incompetence,' he said. 'I feel better myself. So, we are going to be friends?

'Well, of course we are. That is, I think we are. You

might have some irritating faults that I don't know about yet. And I might have faults that irritate you.'

'Not faults, and you don't irritate me. But you can surprise me, I know that.'

'Friends it is, then.' She picked up the second glass of wine he'd ordered. 'We'll go out on occasion, just when we feel like it. You're the best-looking unattached man in the hospital—people will quite envy me.'

'I'm happy to be of service,' he said doubtfully.

'Actually, meeting you is very handy. Last week I had my twenty-ninth birthday and I told my friends I was giving myself a year to get married in. So it's got to be a casual affair with you, hasn't it?'

'It has? Why?'

'Let's face it,' she said judiciously, 'you're not good marriage material, are you?'

He looked at her as if unsure of what to say. 'You're getting at me again, aren't you?'

'Never! I'm being as honest with you as you were going to be with me.'

He drained his glass of red wine and waved to the waiter. 'I'm going to order myself a lemon and lime because I'm driving, but never have I felt more in need of a double brandy. Jane, I've never met anyone like you. You unsettle me. Do you want another drink?'

'I'll have the same as you.'

Once again she noticed his unconscious movement, stroking the tips of the fingers of his left hand across the inside of the fingers of his right. Perhaps he was stressed. 'Let's talk about something other than you and me, shall we?' she asked with a sincere smile.

After that the conversation was enjoyable. David had a quiet, detached sense of humour, quite different from her own more robust sense of fun. Inevitably, they talked shop. He was interested in pain control, a newish branch of anaesthetics, and told her of his hopes to eventually set up a pain-control clinic in the hospital.

'When I took on this job I said I'd only do it if there was a chance of setting up something new. The CEO was quite interested—he's hoping to get me some money to start a clinic. He's asked me to submit detailed proposals. And until then I'll be doing some work on the wards.'

She was curious. 'What have you got in mind?'

'They're very common in America, less so here. You need an interdisciplinary team—properly trained nurses, physiotherapists, physicians, neurosurgeons, anaesthetists, social workers, even psychiatrists. And they've all got to co-operate. Did you know that time off work through back pain costs the country just under four billion pounds a year in lost production? Invalidity benefit for back pain costs just under five hundred million pounds. A good pain-relief clinic will pay for itself in months, not years.'

Jane smiled at his enthusiasm. 'When do you start?'

'In a small way, at once. Would you like to work with me on occasion—if you can be released from Theatre?'

She'd never thought of anything like this. 'Yes,' she said cautiously. 'I think it would be quite interesting.'

Eventually, she had to ask him to take her back. 'But we're enjoying ourselves,' he said. 'Can't I have at least another half-hour of your company?'

She shook her head. 'I've got work to do,' she said.

'At this hour of the night?'

She had told only a few people, but she decided she could tell him. 'I do voluntary work,' she said. 'I'm a Samaritan. You know, if you're suicidal or have personal problems and there's no one you can talk to, you ring up and if you're unlucky you might get me.'

'You're a scrub nurse by day and a Samaritan by night? Don't you see enough trouble in the day?'

'I only do a couple of shifts a week and an occasional weekend. It can be harrowing work, but I get a kick if I think I've helped someone. That makes up for the calls when you think you've done no good at all.'

'I see. We'd better get you back, then. Shall I drive you straight to the office?'

She knew she'd need her own car later so she said, 'No. If you could take me straight home, that would be fine.'

There was little conversation on the trip back, but it was quite amiable. She played another of his tapes—Handel's *Messiah* of all things—while he concentrated on his driving, and it wasn't long before they were outside her house.

He walked her to the front door, where she turned and briskly kissed him. 'I've really enjoyed tonight,' she said. 'We must do it again some time.'

'Wait,' he protested. 'I know we'll be working together tomorrow, but when can I see you again properly?'

She thought for a moment. 'I'm busy for the rest of the week, and I'm playing on Saturday. But we could have a drink in the clubhouse afterwards.'

'Playing?' he asked. 'Clubhouse? You've lost me.'

'I play hockey most weekends.' She kissed him again. 'I'll tell you about it tomorrow. Now, off you go. I don't want to be late.'

She only needed to collect her car keys, and then she was in her Fiesta, heading for the little Samaritans' office. It would be good to listen to other people's problems—she didn't want to think about any she might have herself.

When she got back home, much later, she found Megan in the kitchen, making her late night cocoa. 'How did it go?' she asked.

'Quite a good evening. We had pizza and ice cream.'

'Don't be irritating! You know what I mean. How did you get on with David?'

Jane knew she was going to have to think about this, but she hadn't done so yet. 'I like him quite a lot. But there's something sad about him—I don't know what it is yet.'

'You'll prise it out of him. I'm going to bed. Goodnight.'

Jane made her own cocoa and took it up to her bedroom. She thought about a couple of the calls she'd taken earlier, and wondered if merely listening had helped with anyone's problems. Then she made a decision. She jumped off the bed, took the still unopened envelope from the back of her stocking drawer and opened it. She read it, and once more her face paled. Then she reread it. For an hour she lay on the bed without bothering to get undressed. She knew she wasn't going to sleep.

CHAPTER THREE

IT WAS part of David's pain-relief work out of Theatre, and he had arranged for Jane to accompany him.

'The patient is Lucy Todd,' he told her as they walked along to the ward. 'She's a woman of sixty-nine with a history of reasonable good health until she developed herpes some weeks ago. She had the rash, and then the vesicles appeared in a complete half-girdle round the chest. She knew it was shingles, and was treated with the usual painkillers—atropine ointment was used on the eruptions. Now all signs of shingles have gone—but the pain persists and is as bad as ever.'

'Post-herpetic neuralgia,' she said. 'I've heard of it.'

He nodded. 'I'm going to try drugs to start with—sodium valproate might work. She's been in pain for over eight weeks now and if pain persists over six weeks it's considered chronic. We'll have to try this, but something tells me it won't be too successful. Then we'll use some other form of intervention. I thought perhaps acupuncture.'

She stopped and looked at him in amazement. 'Acupuncture? And you a clinical anaesthetist.'

He smiled briefly. 'Sometimes it works, Jane. And there are never any side effects. It's important not to have a closed mind.'

Mrs Todd *was* in pain, but she came from a generation that accepted it stoically. Jane liked the way David sat by the bed and talked to her. He explained what he was going to do and said that perhaps the drugs might not work.

'We'll try it for a bit, Doctor,' she said. 'We've got to try everything, haven't we? I'm sure you'll get there in the end.'

'Keep smiling, Mrs Todd,' he said, patting her arm.

On the way back to the Theatre suite, he gave her that special smile and said, 'I very much enjoyed our evening and I hope your time at the Samaritans was useful to someone.'

'You never know,' she told him. 'All we're supposed to do is listen. But I like to think it helps.'

He paused, obviously considering what she'd just said. 'I hadn't realised that was what you did. I thought it was some kind of—well, I suppose a social services helpline. I'd like to hear more about it when you've got time to tell me.'

She thought he meant it. He was genuinely curious, and she liked him for it. 'I'll tell you when we have time. And I enjoyed our trip out, too, by the way.'

'So what was this about a drink on Saturday night? More to the point, what are you doing on Sunday?'

'I'll answer the second half first. Sunday is house-keeping day. I do all my washing, ironing, cleaning, letter-writing, bill-paying, polish the car, finish all the little jobs that mount up. It's a date I have with myself once a month. Oh, and I'm going to choir practice.'

'It sounds a full day. And Saturday? What's this about playing hockey and a drink at the clubhouse afterwards?'

Carefully she explained to him where the sports-ground and clubhouse were situated. 'You're welcome to come and watch the match,' she said, 'or just for a drink in the clubhouse afterwards.'

'Could I take you to dinner later?'

'Well, there are hot dogs and pies at the clubhouse. I always stay for a while with my team-mates afterwards—it's expected. But I guess that's not your kind of thing.'

'But I—'

'David, there you are.' Edmund came into the room, wanting to discuss a problem with David. As the two men talked, Jane slipped away.

It was a dank, nasty Saturday afternoon, spitting rain and with a chill wind. Winter seemed to be here already. Some of the players wore tracksuit bottoms to keep warm. Not Jane. Shorts did for her.

She had a good hard game, their opponents coming from a physical training college. After ten minutes of the first half she saw her chance. A badly sliced ball came her way. She dashed down the wing, deftly evading two defenders, and smacked the ball into the net. It was a good goal and she was proud of it.

There was a ripple of clapping from the handful of spectators on the touchline. Jane lifted her stick to acknowledge the applause—and there was David. He was dressed in a long black mac with a slouch hat, but she thought she would know those shoulders anywhere. She felt a warm glow, and waved specially to him. Not many girls had people coming to watch them in this weather.

It continued to be a hard game, though a fair one. Then came a tackle, the crack of sticks meeting and one girl walked away, bent over, clutching her hands together. The referee blew the whistle to halt play and the teams gathered round the injured girl.

'We need a doctor,' muttered the referee.

Jane looked at the now tearful girl's hand. Two fingers were bent backwards at a ludicrous angle, obviously dislocated. From behind her a calm voice said, 'I'm a doctor. May I be of assistance?'

David took the girl's hand in his and gently ran his own fingertips over the backward tilted fingers. 'I'm Dr David Kershaw,' he said to the girl. 'Don't worry, this isn't half as bad as it looks. Now, what's your name?'

'I'm Barbara— Ow!'

'That didn't really hurt, did it, Barbara?'

Barbara considered. 'Well, I suppose not, really,' she said doubtfully. She looked at the injured digits, now in line with their fellows. Without having told her what he was going to do, David had quickly pulled the fingers back into their sockets.

'I don't think you should play any longer. You might like to go to hospital at some stage to make sure nothing is broken, but I'd be surprised if it was. You're going to need physiotherapy too.'

'Great,' said Barbara. 'They teach physios at our college. They can practise on me.'

'Very handy. Now, you might be suffering from shock so go back to the clubhouse, keep warm and drink sweet tea. Any problem, send for me. I'll be here for quite a while yet.'

The coach escorted Barbara off the pitch and the two captains looked at each other. 'Play on?' asked one.

'That's what we're here for.'

They played on, and ultimately Jane's team lost. She didn't mind. She ran over to speak to David. 'David, you came! I'm so glad. Give me twenty minutes to get changed and I'll see you in the clubhouse. Did you enjoy the game?'

'Indeed I did. You looked like a Valkyrie, rushing down the wing. I'm sorry you lost.'

'You don't just play to win, you play to enjoy. And they were good opponents—they deserved the win.'

'Not everyone gets what they deserve,' he said. 'What can I get you to drink?'

'Lager, please. My one indulgence after the match. See you in a few minutes.'

Usually she had a shower and then pulled on a track-suit after the game. After all, she was just going to sit with her friends. This time she wished she had something a bit more, well, attractive to wear. Then she remembered. David was only going to be a friend. Still, she brushed her hair with more than usual vigour.

Jo Gale, a team-mate, scurried back into the changing room out of the bar. 'Jane—that wonderful wonderful man out there says he's waiting for you. Is he your boyfriend?'

'David? Just a man I work with,' Jane said casually. 'I invited him here for a drink.'

Jo groaned. 'I thought it was too good to be true, someone like that on his own. I thought I'd be a bit hospitable and asked him if there was anything I could do for him. And he wants you. I hate you, Jane! Have you got any more men like that at work? Can you bring a selection next week?'

'I'll see what I can do.' Tongue in cheek, she added, 'And thanks for looking after him.'

It took some time for her to get out into the clubroom as her hair took more time to dry than all the others, but she might have guessed. When she finally walked into the bar, there was David, sitting at the end table, with Jo eagerly chatting to him and two more girls with her. David seemed to have the gift of making himself instantly popular.

She walked over and David rose to his feet. She wondered if that was relief she detected in that apparently calm face. 'I got you a drink,' he said, 'and these ladies have been making me very welcome.'

Reluctantly the three stood, said goodbye and left. There were well-understood rules—you didn't interfere with a boyfriend and girlfriend when they first met. Jane grinned and sat at the table, reaching for her drink. 'Did you enjoy the game?' she asked.

As ever, he paused before speaking. 'I don't usually like watching sport,' he said. 'I'm not one of those men who are obsessed by football or cricket. I'd rather play than watch. But I enjoyed watching you. You put a lot into the game, don't you?'

'If it's not worth playing well, it's not worth playing at all,' she told him. 'Do you ever play any team sports?'

He shook his head. 'At school I was a cross-country runner in winter, middle-distance runner in summer. I don't like being part of a team.'

'But we're very much a team at the hospital,' she pointed out. 'You said that yourself. We're all equal.'

'Except for Edmund. He's got a high opinion of himself—and I must say I think it's deserved. Did you see that—?'

Fair was fair. David and Jane had been allowed some time together, but usually on a Saturday night Jane was to be found in one large group or another, having a loud and cheerful conversation about the game. Just because she'd brought the most wonderful man, there was no reason why they should be left alone.

The team captain and coach sat down at their table.

'Hi, I'm Margaret, and this is Louise,' the captain said. 'Thanks for what you did for Barbara, by the way. I'll get you a drink later. Any chance of you turning up regularly? We could do with a doctor actually on the pitch.'

'Sorry,' David said gently, 'but a hospital doctor can never tell when he's going to be needed.'

'Well, you'll always be welcome. Now, I need to borrow your girlfriend for a minute. Jane, they ran rings round our defence this afternoon. We need more strength to get the ball up to you forwards. Who could we move back?'

There followed an intense talk on strategy. Jane had her own definite ideas, and they weren't the same as either Margaret's or Louise's but she had to make her case. After a while she saw a small smile on David's face, but there was nothing she could do about it. This was important. He went to fetch them all a drink.

Slowly the bar began to empty as girls left for dates with boyfriends. Margaret and Louise went to talk to other team members while the older club members began to appear.

'We could go now if you wanted,' Jane said, 'or stay for a few minutes longer. It was nice of you to come and see me. What do you think of the club?'

'The club is fine, and I did take to your team-mates, but I actually came to see you. I came by taxi because I thought I might be able to take you to dinner somewhere. We could have a real drink.'

Jane's face fell—she hadn't thought of that. 'I'm sorry, I really am, but I had an urgent call, asking if I could go and do a shift at Samaritans tonight. I can't get out of it, David, though I really would like to.'

For an instant she saw that he wasn't happy, but he

hid it well. 'It can't be helped,' he said calmly. 'Can you drop me off somewhere in your Fiesta?'

Usually a nurse from the ward assisted the surgeon and anaesthetist when they visited their patients, before seeing them in Theatre. But Ward 7 was short of staff and Jane wasn't needed in Theatre until the afternoon so she accompanied David on his visit.

No one, of course, was anaesthetised before they'd had a very careful examination. Occasionally an anaesthetist would refuse to accept a patient even if the surgeon was willing to operate. Often this was because the patient was obese and the risk of heart failure was too great.

Mostly it was paperwork and very simple investigations. Jane smiled at her first patient, Mandy Wrapp, aged nineteen, who was about to have a lumpectomy. The tumour in the breast was known to be benign. Mandy was already undressed, and Jane fetched the GP's letter with the case history. She had to ask Mandy her name—it was no good just taking it from the notes—and also her date of birth. This information, together with Mandy's hospital number and the name of the consultant, all went onto the plastic band round Mandy's wrist.

Then there were pulse, blood pressure, temperature and a urine sample to take. No allergies, no real previous illnesses, no diabetes, asthma, no regularly taken drugs. Didn't smoke. Nothing to eat or drink since midnight.

Most of this information was already available, but it all had to be checked again. At the same time Jane had to remember not that she had another three patients to see but that this one was a living, worried, human being.

She wasn't merely a case. She was a person. And, in this case, one with an unusual worry.

'This anaesthetic I'm having,' she said uneasily. 'Will it make me talk?'

'Talk? You can't talk, Mandy. You have a sort of gas mask over your face.'

'Well, when I'm coming out of it. I've seen films where people sort of gabble—they say things they don't know they're saying. They ask for people, shout out names. Perhaps they say things. Have you heard them, Nurse?'

'It's just nonsense, usually,' Jane said carefully. She now had some idea where this conversation was going. 'Who's going to be with you from your family, Mandy?'

'My mam. I live with my mam. She's pretty strict, she doesn't know…'

'You don't want her to hear you shouting your boy-friend's name?'

'No. She made me promise never to see him again. Can you keep that mask on me till I'm fully awake?'

'Hardly. But we do try to keep medical confidentiality here, Mandy. I'll pass on your concern to the anaesthetist. We'll do what we can.'

She turned, to find David behind her. 'Dr Kershaw, this is Mandy Wrapp. She has a bit of a problem…'

'That was a hard day but a good one,' David said at the end of the afternoon, stretching to try and ease the tension in his spine. 'Jane, I know you've got an incredibly full social life, but could you spare me, say, a couple of hours straight after we finish work?'

'Are you making fun of me—about my social life?' she asked suspiciously.

'Actually, I'm not. Well, not this time.'

'Then, yes, I'm free until half past eight, then I've got choir practice. Why, what have you got in mind?'

'I'm not going to tell you. The occasional surprise is good for you. Do you have your car today?'

She did in fact, for the day had started out raining and it had continued ever since. 'I'm in the Fiesta.'

'Well, you drive home and I'll follow you. You don't need to change, we're not going anywhere tremendously posh. Well, it's not posh yet.'

'What does that mean?'

'You'll just have to come and find out.'

She couldn't help noticing the difference between her rackety old Fiesta and the smooth ride of the Porsche. 'This is a totally different kind of motoring,' she told him.

He knew what she meant at once. 'I had a Fiesta as my first car when I was a medical student, and I won't hear a word against them. It lasted six years, and only let me down when I neglected it.'

'You don't talk much about your early career, do you?' she said. 'D'you want to tell me about it?'

'Medical student, passed exams, straight into hospital work. Nothing to tell, really.'

But he had left her with the impression that there was something he didn't want to discuss.

They drove for twenty-five minutes after leaving Challis, moving in and out of industrial areas, dodging great lorries. The rain still beat on the windscreen, making the scene even more desolate. Occasionally they caught a glimpse of the river, now jet black and oily-looking, and once they saw the Christmas-tree-light effect of a tanker moving slowly upstream.

Then they swung between two massive stone pillars and into a well-lit forecourt. The bulk of a massive building loomed in front of them. 'Ransome's Wharf,' she said with interest. 'This is where you're buying your flat.'

'I've just got the keys. I thought you might like to look round. And I need some advice.'

As they drove nearer she saw the red brick building with greater clarity. Once it had been a warehouse, but now it had been converted into flats, some already occupied, some not. They drove through a portered front gate and parked the car in the underground garage, before taking a fast lift to the top floor. They walked along a red-carpeted corridor and David unlocked the door of his new flat.

'It's not furnished yet,' he said, 'except for the kitchen, of course. That's got everything. But I've got to buy everything else new. If you don't mind, I'd like a bit of advice on what to buy. I've got nothing of my own.'

Jane's first reaction was one of delight. It would be fun, furnishing a place from scratch. No old pieces too good to throw out but not fitting into the new plan. But then she wondered, Why ask her?

'I don't mind helping,' she said suspiciously, 'but your ideas might be different from mine. After all, we're not setting up home together, are we?'

His answer was as calm as ever. 'No, we're not. But I hope you'll be a guest sometimes.'

He pushed opened the door and switched on the lights. Jane stepped inside, walked across a small hall— and gasped. This was luxury and beauty combined.

The room ran from the front to the back of the building, with windows at each end. One window looked out at the town, the other over the river to the Welsh hills beyond. The curved brick walls had been left as they were, and the floor laid with polished wood.

'Come out onto the balcony,' he said. He opened the double-glazed door, and they stepped into the cold.

She could smell the salt of the river and perhaps the country smell of the distant hills. And she could feel the warmth of his hand on her shoulder. 'This is lovely,' she said. 'You'll be able to sit here and watch the sun go down.'

'If I ever get time to sit. Any ideas about furnishing?' They walked back into the living room.

She had lots of ideas and she'd have loved to furnish this place, but he wasn't to see her enthusiasm. Somehow she felt it would make her vulnerable.

'The proportions of this room are so right,' she said. 'I think you need minimal furniture. Perhaps a set of low bookshelves against that wall. You don't want to spoil the curved line of the ceiling.'

'There are two bedrooms,' he said. 'I thought I'd use the smaller one as a study—computer, magazines, books and so on. A room I can make a mess in.'

'Good idea. D'you want a dining table in here?'

'No. There's a very adequate dining section in the kitchen, and I don't see myself having large, formal dinner parties.'

'So this room is just for relaxing, taking things easy. You'll need a couch, and a chair just for you—perhaps a rocking chair.'

'All in black leather?' he asked, smiling, and she didn't know if he was teasing her or not.

'Very eighties, black leather furniture. You'll turn the place into a typical bachelor pad and have photographers coming round to see how the young man about town lives.'

He winced. 'I'll try corduroy. Or how about a nice floral print and some matching curtains? Something chintzy.'

'You're getting the idea,' she told him.

He frowned. 'Seriously, Jane, I do need advice. What kind of curtains, rugs or carpets? What does colour co-ordination mean? I just don't know. I've never furnished a place in my life.'

She felt herself being drawn in. She really wanted to help him, but she knew it was dangerous. She liked this man, but she had to keep some distance between them. And what could be more intimacy-making than choosing furniture together?

'Let's have a look at the rest of the place,' she said. 'Then perhaps we—or you—can make a few decisions.'

The kitchen was marvellous, superbly fitted and gleaming with state-of-the-art equipment. There was a gas hob, an electric fan oven, microwave, mixer, built-in fridge and freezer—even an electric tin-opener. And to one side a very sizeable dining section. The floor was covered with expensive-looking grey stone blocks.

'You could cater for a wedding in here,' she said.

He looked gloomily at the various items. 'I don't cook,' he said. 'I make sandwiches, buy take-aways and go to the consultants' dining room. I've no idea what to do with half of this stuff, but it came as a package. I could fill that fridge with tins of beer, but that's about all. Are you going to help me set up home, Jane?'

'When I set up home it'll be with someone I'm married to. And I told you, you're not good marriageable material. But I'll give you a hand here and there. Can we see the bathroom now?'

The bathroom was also large and luxurious. There was a big corner bath, a power shower, even a bidet. She looked at this approvingly. But the bathroom walls were of bare plaster. She looked at him enquiringly.

'They'll tile here next week, but I've got to choose a colour.' He took a sample card from the edge of the bath. 'These are the colours on offer. What do you think?'

She knew instantly which colour she would choose, but she didn't say. 'This is going to be your bathroom,' she said. 'You must have some idea. What's your favourite colour?'

'I would have said black but, after hearing what you said about black leather, I'm changing my mind.'

'Thank goodness for that. A black-tiled bathroom would be…' She shuddered.

He looked hopelessly at the samples in front of him. 'Quite frankly, I have no idea. Come on, Jane. I know you picked a colour because I saw you hesitate and smile. Which one is it?'

At first she didn't answer, for she was shocked. She hadn't realised just how perceptive David was, or how easily he could tell what she was thinking. Once again she reminded herself that she would have to be careful with this man. 'I like this blue,' she said.

He took the sample from her, held it against the wall and stood back to look. 'I've seen women do this in shops,' he said. 'I'm not sure what I'm supposed to be looking for, but it seems all right to me. Blue it shall be.'

'Are you sure?' she asked anxiously. 'Don't be persuaded by me.'

'Yes, I'm sure. And who else should persuade me?'

They went to look at the bedrooms. In the smaller

one he wanted to have a folding bed in case he had the occasional guest, but largely it was to be a study, and he knew exactly what he wanted to go in it. The master bedroom was massive, with a walk-in closet for clothes and an abundance of drawer space. Jane thought of her own bedroom, clean enough but always untidy because there just wasn't enough space for all that she owned. This would be like heaven.

'Now I know what luxury is,' she told him. 'I'm very happy sharing with my two friends, but it's nothing like this. When do you move in?'

'In about ten days. They have to finish the tiling, check and clean everything, and then it's just a case of signing the final forms. So I need to start thinking about furniture. You will help, won't you?'

He seemed almost helpless.

'I'll help a bit,' she said, 'but it's got to be your flat. It's not mine, and certainly not ours.'

'You sound like a hard woman, Scrub Nurse Cabot, but I think there's kindness in you somewhere.'

He was stroking his fingers again, she noticed. Was he nervous? She looked at her watch. 'Time's passing. You'd better be taking me home.'

It was fully dark when they drew up outside her house, and the rain was falling harder than ever, rattling on the roof of the car and making the interior seem like a little haven of warmth and comfort. Unusually, he didn't get out and walk round to open her door. Instead, he sat there, he fingers tapping the leather-covered steering-wheel.

'You've made me realise there's more to buying furniture than just getting a catalogue and ordering stuff,' he said. 'You will help me, won't you? Perhaps just with the living room?'

It didn't seem like too much to ask. 'All right, I will,' she said carefully, and then her resistance broke. She giggled. 'I love spending other people's money.'

'Thanks, Jane. You're good to me.' He leaned over, put his arm round her shoulders and bent over to kiss her.

She'd known he would—she'd wanted him to—and it was lovely. When she'd kissed him before, she'd done it deliberately, a hug and a sister-like kiss to show him that they were friends but stop him getting ideas. He'd accepted it with good grace. But now he kissed her and it was so, so different.

She half lay there in the reclining seat, her hands resting in her lap. His fingers ran down the side of her face, curled round the corner of her lip, teased and tickled the sensitive skin. Then his mouth lowered onto hers. She couldn't help it. Her eyes closed of their own accord. She felt a storm of sensations. There was still the patter of rain on the car roof, suggesting the cold and miserable weather outside. But inside she felt warm, contained, safe. Safe…that was an odd word to use when thinking of David Kershaw. But it was how she felt.

There were smells—the expensive leather of the car, his musky cologne, even a hint of the warmth of his body. And there was the feel of him… At first his lips were very soft on hers, merely a passing touch, moving on to her cheek, the corners of her closed eyes and then back to her lips again. This time he was bolder, settling on her, his tongue probing, seeking the inside of her mouth, which had opened without her knowing. She slid her arms round his neck, caressing the crisp curls there, pulling him down to her. For how long they stayed like that she didn't know. All she knew was that she was blissfully happy.

Then his free hand stroked the side of her neck and a fingertip ran across her throat. She didn't want to move—but she had to. Things had gone far enough.

'I'm going to be late, David. I must go,' she whispered.

'Do you have to?'

'Yes. I have to.' He moved away, as she'd known he would. She went on, 'It's choir practice and I swore I wouldn't be late.'

'You don't feel like missing the choir and spending the rest of the evening with me?'

'I might feel like it, but I'm certainly not going to do it. I have to go.' By now she had some of her composure back, and she knew how she had to treat him. 'I'll see you in Theatre, David.'

'No chance of us going out together in the next day or two?'

'Honestly, I've got too much on, too much to do.'

He didn't move so she felt for her doorhandle. Instantly, he was out of his door, opening hers. 'Don't get too wet,' he said. 'See you tomorrow.'

She ran into the house and waited behind the door until she heard the roar of his car engine, slowly diminishing. Then she went up to her room. She needed a shower before she went out. And she needed to think of something else. The memory of that kiss was still with her.

'I suppose I'll be safe with you, shopping in Manchester on Saturday morning,' she said on Thursday afternoon. 'But we'll have an early start, and you've got to get me back in time for the game on Saturday afternoon.'

He'd asked her if she would come with him to pick furniture, and he thought the big stores in Manchester would be the best place to look. 'This trip will be strictly business only,' he said. 'I want nothing but advice on furniture. You will come half as a mother, half as a sister.'

'As long as I get kissed as a mother or sister. If I get kissed at all, that is.'

He looked shocked. 'Some things are not meant to be joked about,' he told her. 'I have feelings for you that are most unfatherly and unbrotherly. But I shall promise to do as you ask. Eight o'clock at your house?'

'I'll be ready. Don't forget your cheque-book.'

It was only half an hour's drive to Manchester and Jane enjoyed the ride. David was as prepared as ever, with a map of the central parking spots and a list of stores they should visit. 'Got them off the Internet,' he told her. 'I could have done my shopping there, too, but I wanted to feel and touch stuff.'

They'd had a long discussion, and he'd decided to buy the minimum at first, then move in and see how he felt. 'Don't even think of buying everything at once,' she'd told him. 'You've got to get the feel of a place. Decide what you really need.'

'You're just being a woman. You want more shopping trips than one.'

He'd meant the remark as a joke, but there was something inside her that acknowledged that there was some truth in the remark. She wanted more time with him, but time when she felt safe.

The first thing they looked for was a bed. 'Single or double?' she asked, then blushed a little. 'Single, of course. What do you need a—?'

'Not only do I want a double bed, I want a king-sized one,' he interrupted. 'Not for any reason that you might think. Just that I'm a big man and I like a big bed.'

'Of course,' she murmured. 'What else could I possibly imagine?'

'And I want a firm mattress.' She decided not to comment.

There was to be no headboard as there was an alcove already built into the bedroom, so the bed was quickly selected. 'What about bedding?' she asked. 'Have you decided on a colour scheme yet?'

'Something to match that blue in the bathroom?' he suggested hopelessly, and Jane realised that this flat was going to be furnished almost entirely according to *her* ideas.

They bought a duvet, pillows, sheets, duvet covers, pillow slips and even a couple of sets of matching towels. All would be delivered shortly, and the builders would accept delivery.

The kitchen was to be next, so they went to another store. Jane suggested that once again he buy the minimum, and add to what he had when he found what he needed, so they chose just a few pots and pans, some cutlery and some crockery. Once again they decided on blue as a unifying colour.

'Anyone would think that you'd never set out to build a home before,' she said. 'And never thought about what you wanted to live with for the rest of your life.'

It had been meant as a little joke, but when he didn't reply she turned to look at him, and his normally placid face was bleak.

'I did set out to build a home once,' he said. 'I didn't get very far.' Then his face brightened. 'I'm fed up with dreary things like bedrooms and kitchens. Let's do the important bit—the living room.'

She wanted to ask him about what he'd said. Usually he was careful and thought before he spoke. But that remark had been spontaneous, almost angry. However, she decided that now wasn't the right time to ask. They'd go to a third store and buy the furniture for the living room.

The builders had given him a sheet with the dimensions of all the rooms and all the windows. Jane suggested they think of curtains first.

'Nothing fancy,' he said firmly. 'I don't like swags or pelmets or anything like that. The function of a curtain is to shut out the light, that's all. In fact, do I have to have curtains?'

'You can't have venetian blinds! You'll think you're still in hospital.'

'But they work.'

Eventually they decided on wooden roller blinds, which would go well with the polished floor and the natural brick.

'Everything so far in that room is very good but plain,' she told him. 'Now, we—that is, you—have got to work out a central theme or colour and work out from there.'

'Ah! I should have been reading those women's magazines that tell you how to plan your home. Are you sure you're enjoying this?'

'Of course I am! I'm doing what every woman wants—planning a home from the very beginning, not having to make do with bits of furniture that have to be made to fit in.'

'Well, I'm enjoying it, too, but it's a bit of a strain

so let's have a break and a coffee. There's a coffee-shop on the next floor.'

'Why are you so well off?' she asked as they sat with a pot of coffee and a most tempting plate of biscuits. 'You seem to be quite happy to spend money.'

He shrugged. 'I guess I've saved much of my salary And I had a…bit of a paying job when I was still a medical student. Apart from my car, I've never spent much. And I get a big rise now I'm a consultant.' He refilled her cup and grinned. 'Aren't you enjoying it, spending my money?'

'Well, yes, I am, I suppose,' she said cautiously, 'but I'm trying desperately to please you and not me. This is to be your home.'

'If it pleases you then I'm sure it will please me. I've got every confidence in you, Jane. Now, did I see you pick up a set of colour cards?'

She *was* enjoying herself vastly, though she wasn't exactly sure why. Dimly, she realised that by getting her to pick his furniture he was binding her to him in a way she found rather unsettling. 'Let's go look at couches,' she said.

They visited two more stores before finding a great curved couch in a dark red fabric. 'It's a good masculine colour,' she told him. 'Now you need a couple of matching scatter rugs on that wooden floor.'

Clutching a scrap of material from the couch—a process he found strange—they went to the floor-covering department and found a pair of Persian rugs in a matching shade, with a pattern she thought she could stare at for ever. They were expensive—but he paid happily.

After that things were simpler. They bought a set of bookshelves, a coffee-table and a rocking chair.

Then it was time to leave so that she could catch the coach for the away game that afternoon.

'I enjoyed the morning,' she said, 'and your flat will look marvellous.'

'Did you feel we were an old married couple?' he asked with a grin.

'No. Certainly not.'

'Well, we certainly haven't done the things that old married couples do. Not yet, anyway.'

He ducked, laughing, as she tried to cuff him. She knew she was blushing. The idea was so attractive.

CHAPTER FOUR

'FRIENDS are for taking advantage of,' Jane told David the following Tuesday afternoon as they relaxed after the day's list. 'My car failed its MOT yesterday and it's in the garage, having major surgery. I've got choir practice late tonight, and I need to get back home from where I'm rehearsing. I could take a taxi, but if you're doing nothing would you pick me up?'

He replied in his customary calm voice. 'I'll do more than pick you up. I'll take you there and then wait to take you home if I can sit in the back of the hall. If I stay any longer in my hospital room I'm likely to go mad.'

'That's kind, but there's no need, David.'

'But I want to. Now, what time shall I pick you up?' In fact, it would save her considerable trouble, so she agreed that he could call for her. After all, she'd do the same for him—or any other of her friends.

'You've got a lovely voice, I know you'd be a wonderful singer,' she flattered him as he drove her to the rehearsal hall. 'Are you sure you won't have a test? It's fun in a choir.'

'It might be fun for you, but I'd hate it. I could no more stand on a stage, singing, than I could play football. I'm a loner, Jane.'

She glanced at his profile, illuminated by the flashes of headlights from oncoming cars. He was so handsome! 'But you work in the theatre already,' she teased. 'You're centre stage there.'

'That,' he told her sternly, 'is different. And Edmund is centre stage. Though I must admit that I'd like to be there.'

The rehearsal was only to last an hour and a half because it was difficult to get all the members together at once as so many hospital staff worked odd shifts. Jane reported to Dan Webster, the obs and gynae registrar, who was organising the concert. David was by her side.

'I'll sit quietly at the back and read my paper,' David said. 'Pay no attention to me.'

He hadn't reckoned on Dan Webster. Dan reminded Jane of a film she'd once seen of a Churchill tank, smashing its way through obstacles. No one sat quietly at the back while there was work to be done.

'David, nice to see you,' said Dan, grabbing him by the hand. 'I'm Dan Webster. Remember, we were introduced a couple of weeks ago? You've brought Jane, have you? Good man. Now, here's a list of choir members. Will you go round them all and find out when they're free next week? Then work out the best time for rehearsals. We need to have at least two meetings, preferably with at least three quarters of the choir present. I'll catch up with you later.'

Jane hid a smile as David looked gloomily at the list and then walked over to the nearest group. 'Hi, I'm David Kershaw,' she heard him say. 'I'm trying to work out rehearsal times for next week.' It was a largely female group. Jane saw interested faces look up, and people gathered round him. Perhaps Dan wasn't a tank after all. Perhaps he was something with a bit more cunning.

'I quite enjoyed that,' David said at the end of the rehearsal. 'I've never been much of a joiner, but I did like working with Dan. And I was very impressed by the singing.' Dan, of course, the minute he knew he had a willing pair of hands, had found all sorts of jobs for David to do. And David was efficient.

'You were impressed by the singing,' Jane said, 'but not enough to try to join us?'

'No. But when I can I'll be happy to help.'

'The eternal cry of the man,' said Jane. 'He won't go on the stage but he's happy to help behind the scenes.' She looked at her watch. 'It was good of you to wait for me. There's half an hour left—can I buy you a drink? Round the corner there's quite a pleasant pub.'

'I'd like that. I'm driving, so it'll have to be two halves of bitter or two glasses of wine. Will the rest of the choir be at the pub?'

She caught his meaning at once. 'All right, we'll go to a pub I know on the way home. Just the two of us. Is that what you want?' She knew it was.

In fact, they didn't like the place. Since she'd been there last a new landlord had taken over. They stopped at the entrance. There was loud jukebox music and the ringing of fruit machines. 'You could come back for a coffee if you like,' she said. 'I don't think much of this place now.'

'I'd much prefer a coffee with you. Let's go.'

It was the first time she'd invited him into the house, and she felt rather shy. Sue was working nights and Megan was out—who knew where. David stood in the kitchen, watching her make coffee, then carried the tray through to the living room. He set the tray by the couch, then waited for her to sit. The lights were dim, as they always were.

There was nothing on TV so she flicked on the CD player without checking what CD was in the machine.

It was Dionne Warwick, singing love songs. 'I like that voice,' he said.

She sat next to him, and they drank coffee and chatted quietly. Both of them were tired. She had let her hair down, and after a while he reached out to it, running his hands through the strands, not pulling but letting the blonde swathe stream over his fingers. She found it calming. Having her hair brushed or stroked had always calmed her. 'Lovely, lovely hair,' he whispered to her.

Then he kissed her. She'd known he would—perhaps she'd wanted him to. This wasn't like it had been in the confines of the car—they had much more room—but he was as gentle as before.

At first she just let him kiss her. She was tired and it was pleasant, soothing almost. But soon she found it was far more than soothing. She wrapped her arms round him, pulling him to her. Her breathing was deeper, the pulse pounding in her wrists, in her throat. Whatever he was doing to her, she wanted more. This man made her feel so alive. Under her tracksuit top she could feel her breasts, pressed against him, become aroused.

She knew he was feeling the same. His breathing, too, was heavy, and she could feel the firmness of his muscles tense against her. His hand stroked her face, her neck. She felt his fingers fasten on the zip on the front of her tracksuit, and the sound as it descended was so tiny and yet so loud.

She knew she could stop him if she wanted to. But she didn't want to. The zip inched its way down to her waist, and she felt the coolness of air on her skin.

Gently, he eased the shoulders of her jacket back, baring more of her skin, revealing the black bra she was wearing. He bent his head further and kissed the side of her neck, then along the length of her shoulder. Her head stretched backwards. It felt so good. The tip of his tongue ran along her shoulder bone, then his lips touched the swell of her breast and she cried out with anticipation. There was nothing she could do to stop him!

Dimly, at the edge of her consciousness, something else was registering. What was that rattling noise? Her brow creased. No, it wasn't important. It couldn't be. Then she heard a voice. 'Hi, there. Anyone at home?'

Megan! That rattle had been the key in the lock!

She jerked upright. David released her and leaned back against the couch, smiling calmly. Hurriedly Jane zipped up her tracksuit and tried to smooth her hair. She reached for a mouthful of cold coffee, and managed to gabble, 'In here, Megan. David and I are having a drink.'

Megan put her head round the door, and David rose to his feet. 'Shall I make us all another drink?' Megan asked.

'I think I should be going,' David said.

'The question is, what d'you think you're playing at?' Sue asked the next night. 'You've been warned against him, you know he hops from one woman to another, you know what he's like.'

'He's very nice,' Jane protested feebly.

'Of course he is! That's how he gets what he wants! There's a long line of women behind him, and each one of them thinks—or thought—that he's very nice.'

Jane said stoutly, 'He'll get nowhere with me.'

She was sitting with her two friends round the kitchen table. It was one of the rare occasions when they were all together, and Sue was determined to make the most of it. 'So what are your intentions?' she asked. 'What do you want—or expect—of him?'

'I really don't know,' Jane confessed. 'I work with him and I know we make a good team. I like his company, and sometimes he seems lonely.'

'Not lonely, just self-contained,' Sue advised. 'I've met men like him before. Mind you, you can't be blamed for falling for him. He is incredibly good-looking.'

'Believe it or not, I'd forgotten that,' Jane said. 'I just like being with him.'

'That's a month or so out of your year gone,' Megan chipped in. 'You've only got eleven months to find a man to marry. Is David going to be the one?'

'Certainly not!'

'Then why are you wasting time on him?'

Sue returned to the attack. 'He has warned you he only wants a casual relationship. That's fine for him. It means he can try like mad to seduce you, succeed, make you desperately unhappy and then just drop you. And his conscience is clear. He warned you in advance.'

'Bit of an old-fashioned word, "seduce",' Jane protested weakly.

'What word d'you think he might use?' Megan asked.

'Look, I just enjoy his company—there's nothing serious between us.'

'Somebody was getting serious when I came in last night,' Megan said primly.

Jane blushed. She hadn't covered up as well as she'd thought. 'Perhaps you're both right,' she said. 'Perhaps I'll keep him at a distance for a while.'

This was, in fact, easier to do than she'd thought. One of the other anaesthetists fell ill and David had to help cover. She had a sudden rush of extra duties, and in between singing in the choir, hockey training and her evenings at the Samaritans she just couldn't see him for well over a week. They met in and outside Theatre, of course, but that was all.

He asked her out several times. 'I know you're busy, but I think you could find some time for me,' he said reproachfully when they were scrubbing up in the anteroom.

'I've got a full life, you know that. And don't forget, you wanted a casual relationship.'

He looked gloomy. 'If I remember right, you said that, not me. But I suppose you're right.'

He didn't know just how much that remark hurt. The hurt surprised her, too.

Four days later he asked her if they could have a talk. As ever they were in greens, drinking the inevitable coffee. 'Do you know Sister Greta Fallows?' he asked.

'Yes, I know her casually. She's Night Sister on Ward 15.'

Jane guessed what was coming, but she tried not to let it show. There wasn't a reasonable-looking, unattached man in the hospital that Greta hadn't been out with. And a few attached men, too. She had dyed black hair and wore rather a lot of lipstick. Sue had once had an argument with her, and had described her afterwards as the sort of woman a man thought he fancied when he'd had far too much to drink. Then Megan, who was normally pleasant about everyone, had remarked that her figure was a great tribute to the art of the corsetière. It was nice to be catty occasionally.

She decided to save David a little embarrassment. 'She's asked you out,' she said. 'Where to?'

He still managed to look calm. 'She has asked me

out, as a matter of fact,' he said. 'She's unexpectedly been given a couple of tickets for a concert in Manchester next Saturday night, and has no one to go with.'

Jane snorted. 'Do you believe that story?'

David sighed. 'I suppose not. But she seemed very pleasant.'

'Are you going to go with her?'

'Well…I don't yet know many people here. And you don't seem to have much time. I haven't seen you for over a week now. D'you mind?'

She smiled agreeably. 'What you do is your own concern. Since ours is only a casual affair, you can obviously do what you like. As can I.'

He looked at her broodingly. 'You're being too nice, too reasonable,' he said. 'It makes me suspicious. Actually, the concert is one I'd like to go to. But I must say, I'd rather go with you.'

'You go if you want to,' she said flatly. 'Look, David, I won't mess you about. I'm not sharing a man with anyone, it's too much like hard work. We'll stay friends, but if you go out with her you don't go out with me.'

She watched as he closed his eyes, as if in pain. Then he opened them and smiled. 'I thought you were sweet. And so you are, so sweet as steel. OK, I'll tell her I can't make it. I don't want to lose you.'

'You can't lose me,' she pointed out with a grin. 'You haven't got me.'

He shook his head in exasperation. 'I've never met—'

A junior nurse put her head round the door and said, 'Mrs Snell is waiting for you, Dr Kershaw. I'm afraid she's in a bit of a state.'

'Right, I'm on my way. Mustn't keep Mrs Snell waiting, must we?'

Only when he'd left did Jane breathe out a long sigh of relief. Did David guess that her apparent lack of caring was only a front? Then she caught herself. She *couldn't* allow herself to care. She *couldn't* fall for David Kershaw. Their affair was entirely casual.

Later that evening Jane got a phone message from the hockey team captain. The Saturday home match had been cancelled because their opponents couldn't field a team, so Saturday afternoon was free. Only for a minute did she hesitate, and then she phoned David's extension at the hospital.

'David Kershaw.' She'd only seen him a few hours ago, and yet the sound of that voice still gave her a thrill. What was she doing?

'This is Jane,' she said. 'Look, this isn't a consolation prize for giving up Sister Fallows, but I've just heard that I'm not playing on Saturday afternoon. If you've nothing else arranged, would you like to spend the afternoon with me? We could go out.'

'I'd love that. I've got to be back in the evening, though. I'm on call. Still, I only have to be twenty minutes away. What d'you fancy doing?'

'Liverpool is only half an hour away in that passion wagon of yours. Let's go and be tourists.'

'I'd like that. Goodnight, sweetheart.'

He'd called her 'sweetheart' for the first time. She wondered if he'd meant anything special by it.

It was exciting, waiting for David to pick her up at Saturday lunchtime. She felt like a teenager on her first date, not like an old experienced woman of twenty-nine. But she liked the feeling.

'You know what you're doing?' Sue had asked her.

'I guess so. Whatever I'm walking into, I'm walking into it with my eyes open.'

Sue hugged her. 'Good luck to you. And, incidentally, not only do I think he looks fabulous, I hear he's got a good heart as well. He spent quite a bit of time on our ward yesterday, helping one of the trainees. He didn't have to, it wasn't his job—he just did it.'

'Yes,' said Jane. 'He can be thoughtful.'

She had dressed carefully—still trousers of course, for there was no way she could wear a skirt and get out of his car elegantly. But instead of her usual black, these trousers were a light grey, and she matched them with a smoky blue cashmere jumper. In case it got cold she added her ever-reliable fleece.

He was on time. Jane watched the car pull up from the living room window, and ran to the front door before he had chance to ring the bell. All right, it showed that she'd been looking out for him, waiting for him, but she didn't care.

'You look good,' he said, 'but, then, you always do.'

'Thank you, kind sir. All compliments gratefully received. D'you want a coffee or shall we get straight off?'

'Let's go. I've never been to Liverpool, and I'm quite looking forward to it.'

As they drove he was quieter than he usually was, and she didn't think it was because of the traffic. Driving was easy here. 'You're a bit reserved today,' she said. 'Not your usual self. Is anything wrong?'

He shook his head and smiled briefly. 'Not really. I'm playing things carefully. I made one mistake with you, and I don't want to make another.'

Impulsively, she leaned over to kiss him on the

cheek. 'I'll let you know if you're making a mistake. Just be your normal self.'

They drove alongside the river, and eventually stopped in a vast parking lot at a place called Albert Dock. Then they wandered round, hand in hand, like tourists. She liked holding his hand.

The Albert Dock had once been a set of great red-brick warehouses round a central basin. Now the upper floors had been converted into flats and offices, and there were shops, cafés and pubs at ground level. There was a TV studio, a maritime museum and a branch of the Tate Gallery. 'I'll show you the lot,' she said enthusiastically. 'Art gallery first.'

There was a lot to see and they only had half a day so the gallery didn't take long. 'I think a lot of it is rubbish,' she said, 'but I like those drawings. Come on, we'll go to the maritime museum now.'

The maritime museum was more fun. They looked at engines, great models of liners, famous sea pictures. The most interesting part was a reconstruction of a Liverpool street and the hold of a ship, where emigrants went steerage class to America. 'Better by Concord,' he said. There was too much to see so they kept their tickets and decided to come again.

Lastly, she walked him past the famous Liverpool waterfront onto the ferry, and they sailed across the Mersey. It was getting colder now, and she needed her fleece. But they looked at the Liver birds, watched the gulls screaming and diving, and saw the great ships moving down the channel to the sea.

'A hundred years ago, most of the world's shipping was registered on the banks of this river,' she told him. 'It isn't now.'

'Things change, Jane. Even people change.'

She wondered if he was trying to tell her something.

The ferry bumped back against the dock, where it was moored with nonchalant ease, and then they walked back to the Albert Dock. They sat, outside a café, and had a coffee and a large roll each.

'My feet and legs hurt,' she said, rubbing her calves vigorously. 'All this enjoyment is tiring.'

He smiled. 'I like going out with you, Jane. Everything you do, you do enthusiastically. I've really enjoyed this afternoon.'

She was honest. 'I like being with you, too.' Then she grinned and went on, 'Apart from anything else, you're so good-looking that other women look at me and feel jealous, and I like it.'

He looked uncomfortable. 'I don't know if that's true. But certainly men feel jealous of me. You're the most…radiant girl here.'

'Radiant?' she asked. 'I like that.'

He went to fetch them both another coffee, and she mused over what they'd both said. Perhaps men *did* look at her, but certainly more women looked at him. It happened all the time at the hospital. Even now, as he was queueing, she saw a young girl's head turn. He was gorgeous. But he didn't seem overly aware of it. He didn't preen all the time, like some good-looking men she'd seen.

He returned with their coffee. 'So you just go out with me because I'm good-looking? And I thought it was my brain, not my body, you were interested in.'

He was joking, of course, but she answered him seriously. 'Life is too short to go out with a man just because of his looks. No, personality is far more important.'

Together, they stared at the floating island in the middle of the dock. It was a representation of the British Isles, used in television weather forecasts.

'I'll tell you a secret if you promise not to tell anyone else.' He was half laughing, and she was instantly intrigued.

'I love secrets. At least, I think I do. It's not something you've done that's a bit…doubtful?'

'I think perhaps it is. I certainly wouldn't want anyone at the hospital to know.'

She was worried a little at first, but then she saw he was still laughing. 'Come on! You can't tease me like this. Tell me what it is, and I promise to stand by you.'

'Promise? I'll hold you to that.' He leaned across the table and lowered his voice. 'This is the story of when I was an impoverished medical student, living on baked beans and Scotch eggs. I desperately needed money. I wanted to buy a little car, a Fiesta like yours. And I was offered quite a substantial sum…if I would sell my body.'

'If you would *what*?'

'If I would sell my body. Well, lend it, anyway. I got a job as a male model.'

'A male model! As in walking down the catwalk with your hand on your hip?'

He winced. 'Not exactly that. I mostly did magazine illustrations and that kind of thing. It could have been quite lucrative. My agent was bitterly disappointed when I told her I wasn't going to do any more.'

She couldn't help laughing. 'You! A model! Standing under spotlights and looking thoughtful, and romantic, and debonair, to order. Is that what you did?'

'I'm afraid so. There were too many photographers who weren't content just to take a picture that would sell sweaters. They wanted to produce great art.' He laughed reluctantly. 'But I got my car out of it.'

'Why did you stop, then? It sounds like a good idea to me. I'd have done it while I was training if I'd had the chance.'

'Ah. There I was, a new doctor, hoping to learn. White coat, stethoscope dangling round neck, book of instructions in pocket. I was asked to fetch a patient from the waiting room. And I found her staring at a magazine with a large picture of me inside the back cover. She looked at the magazine, looked at me, looked at the magazine again and decided she was imagining things. I decided to avoid future possible embarrassment and gave up the job. My agent wasn't pleased.' He stayed silent, thoughtful for a moment, then said, 'Now you know the guilty secrets of my past, tell me about yours.'

'I've got no secrets,' she said promptly, and hoped he'd believe her. She could tell him perhaps—but not yet.

He looked thoughtful again. 'I like you a lot, Jane,' he said, 'and I think you like me. We get on well together. So why do you treat me in such an offhand manner?'

'You mean, why aren't I head over heels in love with you? Why aren't I besotted? I could be, but I won't allow it to happen. You're good company but all you want is a casual relationship. That's fine by me. You're not good marriageable material and some day I want to get married and have children.'

'And if you find a suitable man while you're seeing me?' he asked softly.

She found it hurt to give him an honest answer. It felt brutal, but she knew she had to. 'Then goodbye you,' she said. 'Just like you said goodbye to I don't know how many girls at Lady Mary Hospital.'

'Ow,' he said. 'Are you the woman who counsels for the Samaritans? God knows what advice you give.'

'It's good,' she told him. 'I went on a course. And we don't exactly counsel, we listen.' She was silent for a moment, but she could tell by the thoughtful way he was looking at her that he wanted her to continue. 'Being a Samaritan teaches you something about relationships. You hear what difficulties people get into, and you sympathise. But it teaches you the necessity of being…not hard, but determined. You don't want to make the mistakes that other people have made.'

'Everyone makes mistakes at some time,' he told her, and she could tell that he meant it.

'You're not as hard as you pretend,' she said. 'When you're nervous or thoughtful—like now—you rub the inside of the fingers of your right hand with the fingertips of your left hand.'

'You've noticed!' He looked down at his hands and drew them apart. 'I don't know why I'm surprised,' he said. 'I know you're a subtle person.' He held his right hand, palm upwards, towards her. 'Look at my fingers.'

She'd held his hand quite often, but now she examined it. It was hard to detect at first, but along the sides of his fingers she saw the tiny scars that indicated surgery. 'What happened?' She looked at him questioningly.

He stared down morosely at his hand, flexed it, twisted it, touched the fingertips together. 'There's enough movement, enough sensitivity, enough dexterity for anaesthetics,' he said, 'but not enough to enable me to be a surgeon. Which was what I wanted to be.'

She took the hand, squeezed it gently and for a moment brought it up to her lips to kiss. 'Come on,' she said, 'you're going to tell me the story.'

He took his hand from her and poured them both more coffee. She thought she'd never seen him look so bleak. She said nothing, realising that he was getting his thoughts together, working out how—or what—to tell her. She knew that in his own time he would tell her.

'I was engaged once,' he told her, 'to a girl called Diane Furling.' He still didn't look at her, his eyes fixed somewhere across the water. 'She had nothing to do with medicine—which perhaps was the problem. In fact, she was the director of the firm I modelled for. She got me my first break.' His eyes came back to Jane. 'She was nothing like you—she seemed to live on a diet of Perrier water and lettuce leaves.'

Jane's eyes fell on the crumbs of the roll she had just eaten. 'Am I supposed to take that as a compliment?' she asked.

He smiled wryly. 'Yes, you are. Because it was meant as a compliment. Anyway, Diane was always beautifully groomed. She would never run, get out of breath, anything like that. She hated medicine, but did think that if I stuck to it I ought to become something like a cosmetic plastic surgeon. She knew one who might offer me a job when I was fully qualified. We mixed with a very upmarket crowd—TV, stage and so on. I quite took to it all.'

By now his voice was entirely cynical. 'I guess I was a bit overwhelmed by it all. She suggested I give up medicine, said I could make a fortune with my face. I told her no thanks. Anyway, we went to this party. She drove—she absolutely refused to get into my Fiesta. Her car was a Porsche.'

Jane looked at him, amazed. 'But you've got one now!'

'I know. I like it, it's a good car. In fact, I bought it on purpose, because there are some demons you've just got to lay. But…I thought she was fit to drive after the party because I knew she hadn't had anything much to drink. Fattening, you know. What I didn't know was that she'd been scoring cocaine in the Ladies. In those days I was a bit naïve. She wasn't fit to drive. We took a corner far too quickly, she lost control and we crashed and turned over. The car was a write-off. She was shocked, scared, but unhurt. I was concussed. That was bad enough as I woke up in my own hospital. Then I found my right hand bandaged. My fingers were broken, and there was nerve damage.'

He stopped and looked down at where he was unconsciously rubbing the damaged fingers. She said nothing. 'The hospital got the best orthopaedic men there were, but they never managed to restore full feeling and flexibility. I wanted to be a surgeon. I was told I could be a competent one—doing the smaller, less important operations—but I would never be in the first class. So I transferred to anaesthetics, which I very much like.'

There was silence for a minute. 'And Diane?' she asked.

'Came to see me in hospital, quite unrepentant. Said it didn't matter about the fingers, they wouldn't show on photographs. She had no idea of what I was feeling. She had been offered the biggest contract she'd ever had for me. I was to give up medicine, go to America and be the centre figure in a new range of men's cosmetics. I would become a millionaire. I told her I didn't want to be a millionaire, I wanted to be a doctor. She gave me my ring back, told me she objected to wearing cheap jewellery and when I came to my senses to get in touch with her. I never did.'

Jane tried to get a grip on her whirling emotions, and said, 'I hope you're not expecting me to say I feel sorry for you.'

He grinned at her. 'Well, I did wonder. I guess I should have known better.'

'All right, you had a hard time with this girl, though it strikes me you were well rid of her. I'm sorry about your fingers. But you had no right to think all women were the same. It was just an excuse to avoid commitment in the future, and I suspect you were getting your revenge for what just one person had done to you. Some of those women you told you only wanted a casual relationship with…you hurt them, David.'

Now he was angry. As always, he was calm, but she could see the spark in his eye, and there was a thickness to his voice that hadn't been there before. 'Have you ever thought it a bit too easy to sit in an office, answering the phone, listening to people but not judging?'

'You have to be detached,' she told him.

'Other people's problems are easy to bear.'

She stood. 'I think it's time we were going.'

They drove back in silence, her mind churning. It was getting dark and he had to be near the hospital because he was on call that evening. Halfway home she put her hand on his arm. 'Will you pull into that lay-by?'

'May I ask why?' His voice was cold, intending to hurt.

She took a breath. 'Because I ask you to,' she said impatiently. 'Come on, it's not much to ask.'

He did pull in and switched off the headlights. They were on top of a small hill, facing myriad factory lights, but beyond they could see the dark silver of the river.

She undid her safety belt, leaned across to take his face between her hands and kissed him. 'I've been thinking about what I said. You were right. I was crass, insensitive and wrong. I've never had any real ambition that I haven't achieved, and so I can only guess how hard it was for you. I'm sorry.'

He laughed and shook his head. 'No, it's me that should be sorry. You're good for me, Jane. What you said hurt because I thought you were right. The idea just took some getting used to. Come on, we're friends now.'

Then he kissed her. It was very nice but it was a strain as their bodies had to contort. 'These cars weren't designed for kissing in,' he said.

'Then let's go somewhere else.'

CHAPTER FIVE

JANE had never been to David's room at the hospital. From six o'clock he was on call, and if there was an emergency he had to be able to get to Theatre within twenty minutes. It was most unlikely that there *would* be an emergency, but the hospital management needed to have someone on standby.

They did think of going to a pub near the hospital entrance, but neither of them fancied it much. 'I can make you a drink,' he told her. 'I've even got the makings of a sandwich in the communal fridge.'

'Just a drink, I think,' she told him. 'I'm still full from that roll we had.' So he left her in his room to fetch it.

It was a typical hospital room, and she had been in many in her time. It was plain but serviceable. There was a bed, desk, cupboards, wardrobes and drawer space. On his bookshelf she noticed textbooks on surgery—the knowledge she now had gave them an added poignancy.

There was only one easy chair so she took off her shoes and sat on the bed. 'There are no personal touches in this room,' she told him when he came back with two steaming mugs. 'No pictures, no music.'

'A definite and deliberate policy. At Lady Mary I had a doctor's flat, quite a bit bigger than this. It was furnished, but I had some stuff of my own. I put it all into storage because I thought that would make me look harder for a proper place of my own. And you helped me furnish it, Jane. I decided that once I was a consultant I'd grow up. Get a proper place to live and—'

'And alter your lifestyle?' She grinned. 'Stop being a perpetual medical student?'

'Something like that,' he confessed. 'I wanted to be respectable at last.'

'What a dreadful ambition!'

She was sitting cross-legged at the head of his bed. He offered her a mug of tea, then kicked off his own shoes and sat the same way at the other end of the bed so they faced each other.

'You told me about your medical life,' she said. 'What about the rest of it? Are your parents still alive?'

'Very much so. Dad's a retired doctor. I have a brother who's a GP in New Zealand and he's married to another GP. They've got two little kids, Frederica and David, who's named after me. Ma and Pa are out there now, technically visiting but actually working as full-time babysitters. They love it.'

'Have you been out there yourself?'

'I visited them last year. I wanted to get to know my niece and my nephew. Actually, I was offered a job there but I wanted to stay in the UK. We keep in touch every week by e-mail.'

'It's sad to have a family so far away, but nice to know that they love you and want to keep in touch.'

Both were silent for a minute, busy with their own thoughts.

'A personal question, Jane. You know a lot about me. I want to know something in return.'

'Ask away,' she said cautiously. 'I'll answer…if I can.'

'Why have you never married? I would have thought you'd have been snapped up long ago.'

She hesitated. She could give some smart answer about still waiting for Mr Right—she didn't have to be completely honest.

'You can trust me, you know,' he said softly.

She was still undecided. *Could* she trust him? This was a wider question than the one he'd asked. She made up her mind. Yes, she could.

'All right. I nearly was married once—in fact, I was engaged and lived with a doctor for over two years. His name was John Gilmore, and this was some time ago. I thought we were happy. Both of us were working very hard. We talked vaguely of marriage, but never got round to doing anything about it. John was an neurologist, working for his FRCS exams. We had a little rented flat—this was in Leeds.'

'What went wrong?'

'Nothing really went wrong. He passed the FRCS and was offered a wonderful job in the States, in Boston. He had to take it. I went over to be with him after three months. I got a job and stayed for a year, but I just didn't like the life and I came home. We tried to live on two different continents, but it didn't work. We phoned each other less and less, and after a while he came over to see me. He'd met someone else over there. So we parted, but stayed good friends.'

'It was good of him to come over to tell you in person. What did you feel afterwards?'

She decided to be honest with him. 'As a matter of fact, I was a bit relieved. The time that I had with him—it was good, but I guess it wasn't good enough.'

'Always hold out for the best,' he said. He went on, 'But that's not your entire story, is it? There's more. Everyone thinks that good old Jane is cheerful, hard-working, outgoing. But I think there's a bit of wariness hidden somewhere. What are you hiding, Jane?'

He was much much shrewder than she'd ever guessed. She would have to be careful with him, even thought there was no great mystery.

'I never knew my parents,' she said. 'I was only told that my mother was a student at a teacher training college who just couldn't cope with me. I was adopted, and made very happy by the lady whose name I carry, Alice Cabot. She was everything a mother could be— loving, kind, encouraging. After she'd had me six years she adopted another child, a boy who became my brother Peter. She asked me first and even though I was so young we talked about it carefully. And the three of us got on very well.'

She stopped and took a great mouthful of tea. 'When Peter was seventeen and I had just qualified, our mother died. Just like that—a stroke, a couple of weeks in hospital and then she was dead. We were devastated, but somehow we survived and Peter has trained to be a doctor. He's a house officer in London. Although we're apart, we're still very close—if you see what I mean.'

'I see what you mean. I think he's a very lucky young man. But there's more, isn't there, Jane? You're keeping something back.'

'Yes,' she said slowly. 'I'm keeping something back.'

There was silence for a while, then he said, 'I can act like a Samaritan if you like. Imagine I'm on the other end of a telephone line, and just tell me—you might feel better. But if you don't want to, I certainly won't pry.'

She remained silent, and he said nothing more.

When she thought she was ready, that she could control her voice, she said, 'There's a letter at the back of one of my drawers upstairs. It's worried me more than any letter I have ever received. And I don't know what to do about it. I've never been undecided like this, ever.'

'Do you want to tell me who it's from?'

This was the crux. And to her surprise, she found she did want to tell him. She certainly couldn't tell Peter and she hadn't been able to talk to Sue or Megan, so why this man? But she would tell him.

'I told you I was adopted, apparently about six weeks after birth. It was all done properly through an agency and, as I said, I couldn't have had a better mother. But now…but now I've just had a letter. It came from the adoption society, and apparently my real parents want to get in touch with me. It was an official letter—my parents don't know my name or address. The adoption society will forward any messages I want to send back. If I don't want to get in touch, that's fine.'

'When did you get the letter?'

'A few weeks ago. I don't know what to do. For the first time in my life I really don't know what to do.' She knew her voice was tremulous, but there was nothing she could do about it.

'Just talk about it,' he said. 'You don't have to make sense, just talk about it. No one's going to judge you or make you take a decision. Just talk.'

Just talk. Was it as easy as that?

'I told you I had a happy childhood—it couldn't have been better. She was my mother, I still think of her that way. My…real mother gave me up. And where did my father just appear from? What was he doing before? He gave me up, too. I don't need parents now. Once you've got them, you can't un-get them. But…I am their child. Some of the stories I've heard in Samaritans are about people with dreadful difficulties. Giving me up might not have been my real parents' fault. And what else don't I know? I might have a brother or sister—I love Peter dearly, but I'd like that. But what if we didn't get on?'

There were tears rolling down her cheeks and he handed her a handkerchief but very wisely made no move towards her.

'The top and bottom of it is I don't know what to do, and I'm frightened.'

'Is there any hurry?' he asked. 'They waited for years to get in touch with you, so a week or two longer won't hurt. Wait until you feel that you know what to do. Then do it.'

She thought about that. It wasn't exactly advice, but it was worth listening to. 'Now I know what good the Samaritans do,' she said. 'I do feel better for having told you.'

'I'll fetch us more tea,' he said. As he went she realised that he was giving her time to settle down, to compose herself. He was a thoughtful man.

'It's warm in here,' she said a few minutes later. All hospital rooms were warm, and those in the residency were no exception. Jane crossed her arms and pulled off the blue cashmere sweater. Underneath she was wearing a sleeveless white blouse.

'You've got good arms,' he said. 'They're nurse's… hockey-player's arms. No fat, just enough muscle to be slightly rounded. I like them.'

'Thank you, sir,' she said, 'and thank you for the tea.' She had just finished it.

He wriggled up the bed so that their knees were touching and they could look at each other face to face. She couldn't back away—her back was against the wall—but she decided she didn't want to anyway.

She stared at those dark blue eyes, for some reason now even darker. She stared at those curved, those very kissable lips. She had half forgotten how really handsome he was because now that he was her friend she saw the friendship before the good looks. But was he more than a friend?

He leaned forward, took her hand and held it up, gently running his fingers along the inside of her naked arm. The caress was gentle, but strangely effective. She wouldn't have thought that the inside of her arm would have been so sensitive. She closed her eyes.

They were still facing each other. She felt his hands reach to her shoulders, the fingers on top, stroking the sensitive side of her neck, his thumbs touching her cheeks. It was so soothing.

'Let me sit beside you,' his gentle voice urged.

She didn't open her eyes, but she eased herself to the side of the bed and felt him move beside her. She slid further down the bed, stretching her legs out. His arm came round her shoulders and she half turned to nestle against him.

He bent over to kiss her. She knew what was happening, what was going to happen. She wanted it to happen. She liked—loved—David. No, her feelings for him were confused. But definitely she wanted this to happen. She was twenty-nine, able to make up her own mind, not a foolish young girl. She giggled.

'And what are you laughing at?' he asked, his voice soft, amused.

'I was thinking that I was going into this with my eyes open, but I've got them closed.'

'So you're happy? No worries at all?'

'I'm perfectly happy.'

She felt him move against her, felt the delicate touch

of his lips on first one eyelid then the other. 'Yes,' he breathed, 'your eyes are closed.'

Then he was kissing her and it seemed to go on for ever. She slid further down the bed and he slid with her. She felt at ease, perfectly happy.

His fingers ran down the front of her blouse, popping open the buttons one by one. She shivered as the tips touched her skin, stroked the swell of her breasts. She wasn't going to be a passive partner—if she was giving herself she would give herself wholeheartedly. Her arms stretched up round his neck and she pulled him against her. Now they were side by side, facing each other, and his tongue touched the inside of her lips, then moved deeper.

He continued to stroke her. His hand was now under her blouse, and she sighed with delight as he ran his hand up and down her spine. With a deft movement he undid her bra, and the release felt good. She sobbed with passion as he dipped his head to her freed breasts and took each into his mouth in turn. Her body seemed to be burning, the urgent desire flashing between her lips, her breast and her loins. She knew that she wanted him as much as he wanted her. Now her hands were underneath his shirt, feeling the hard warmth of his body. Their clothes were in the way, they should—

The phone rang.

Both stopped, their bodies frozen with shock. The phone didn't stop ringing. She looked at it, a hateful black plastic object on his bedside table. It was still ringing.

'You're on call,' she said, her voice hoarse. 'Answer it.'

'But, Jane…'

'You know you have to. If you don't they might send someone round.'

He leaned back and picked up the receiver. She heard a tense, 'Yes?'

There was a pause. She was looking at his face now and she saw the raw emotion drain away, to be replaced by a more impassive look. He snapped, 'I understand. I'll be there in exactly fifteen minutes. You've sent for Mr Steadman?…Good.'

He replaced the receiver and swung his legs so he was sitting on the edge of the bed, his head bowed. She sat upright to put her arms round him from behind. There was a sweet sadness in the way her breasts pushed against his back.

'No, there isn't time,' she said, 'and I feel as badly as you do. But sit here for just a minute and kiss me.' She wriggled to sit beside him.

It was a different kind of kiss. She could feel the passion still there, but both of them knew there was nothing they could do about it. After a while she pushed him away, and reached behind her back to fasten her bra.

'Time for you to move, Dr Kershaw,' she said with a wry smile. 'I should splash some cold water on your face. You look as if you've been…enjoying yourself.' Then she started to button up her blouse. She didn't want to look at his face again so she kept her head down. He didn't move.

'Come on, David, you're a professional, just as I am. Time to go to work. How long are you going to be?'

He shrugged. 'I'll be honest. It's an emergency Wertheim's hysterectomy, but we don't know how far the carcinoma has spread so it could go on for hours. You don't want to stay and…?'

She shook her head. 'You know that wouldn't be a good idea.' She added mischievously, 'For a start, you wouldn't be able to concentrate on what you were doing. No, David, I've had a lovely day, and we nearly had a wonderful ending. But I'd better go home now.'

'I suppose you're right. What about tomorrow?'

She smiled at him sadly. 'I did tell you, I'm going on a course for a week, over at Leeds University. It's on new techniques of Theatre management. But I'll be back next weekend. Will you phone me while I'm away?'

'Of course I will. Look, d'you want to stay here a while? I can't even take you home.'

'No problem. It's not too late—I'll get a bus or a taxi. Come on, I'll walk across to the hospital with you.'

Jane took a taxi home. She felt unsure of herself—the interrupted evening with David had unsettled her more than she'd realised. It wasn't just that they'd been stopped from… It was a lot of things.

Almost always she went out on Saturday nights. Usually she went to the club and she thought about telling the taxi to drive there now, but decided against it. She liked company, but company at the club wasn't what she needed right now. She almost persuaded herself that she needed to prepare for the course that started on Monday, but she knew it wasn't true. She'd already read the books and articles they'd asked her to.

It would have helped if her friends had been home, but neither was there. Irritated, she flung about the house for twenty minutes, then went upstairs and ran herself a long bath. Usually she had a shower—it was seldom she allowed herself time for a bath. But tonight she had more time than she knew what to do with. She could always ring the Samaritans and ask if they needed an extra hand. No, not tonight. She wasn't fit to listen to other people's problems. She had her own. She would sit and soak.

She poured large amounts of foam bath into the water. It belonged to her friends but she knew they wouldn't mind. Then she undressed. For a moment she caught sight of her naked body in the full-length mirror, and a thought flashed through her mind. That body could have been... She blushed, and lowered herself into the bath.

After a while the hot water soothed away some of her anguish, the foam relaxed her and she felt a bit better then she had. She knew she had to think about things. For a start, why was she in such a state?

She had nearly let David Kershaw make love to her. Make love to her? What had love to do with it? He'd never said he loved her. They'd talked about what he wanted at the Black Lion—in fact, she'd mentioned it first. A casual affair.

So why had she gone with him so readily? If not a virgin, she certainly wasn't given to casual sex. For her, sex was part of a much wider relationship. Why had she, tough Jane, a match for any man, so readily given way to David Kershaw? No, it hadn't been giving way. She'd been as eager as he.

Jane liked David. She enjoyed his company, they were friends. There was a question she was being drawn towards, but she didn't want to think about it, she didn't want to have to answer it. But she would have to. Did she love David? Had she become one of the women fatally attracted to him, who later paid the price for their love? It looked like it. So should she give him up? It made sense when she knew he wasn't going to marry her.

The minute she thought of giving him up, she felt desolate. It wasn't what she wanted. She couldn't give him up—no matter what it cost her. And she wouldn't sit here and mope. It was still quite early. She climbed out of the bath, dressed and walked out to her car. She would drive to the clubhouse and find some company.

Jane enjoyed the course. It was always interesting to meet people from other hospitals, who did the same things but often in different ways. And the course content itself was very good—she decided she'd write a memo to the hospital management committee and ask Edmund Steadman if he would support her proposals. She thought he well might.

And Leeds was her old stamping ground. She revisited the places she'd known when she'd lived there with John Gilmore. The pub they used to drink in was still there, but the ward she'd worked in had changed completely. The building that housed the little flat they'd lived in had been completely renovated, and their flat no longer existed. That was symbolic, she realised. These days she seldom thought of John, and when she did there was no longer that catch at the heart, that momentary hurt. He had passed out of her life. She thought of David more.

But had John been replaced by David? Was she asking for more heartache? She didn't know.

He rang her at the end of her first day on her mobile and she told him the number of her room extension for the future. They could talk longer that way. And she liked hearing from him.

'It's a good group of people,' she told him. 'We're being worked very hard, and I'm now in the bar, having a bit of a post-mortem on what we've learned so far.'

'Enjoy yourself. Are there any lovely men there?'

'Don't ask for compliments,' she told him. 'It doesn't suit you. And, yes, there are lots of lovely men here.'

'Oh, I see. What's your room like?'

'It's a lot better than yours. It's *en suite*.'

She could hear the laughter in his voice. 'So my room didn't give you happy memories?'

'Well, sort of. Some happy memories certainly. But I had the feeling of being saved by the bell—telephone bell this time.'

This time he laughed out loud. 'Funny. I feel just the opposite. Jane, it's good to hear your voice. Shall I ring again in a couple of nights?'

'I'd like that,' she said honestly. 'I'd like that very much.'

Actually, he rang every night, and she looked forward to his calls. They had cheerful, noncommittal conversations. He told her that the scrub nurse who was taking her place wasn't half as competent as she was, and Edmund Steadman was getting noisily furious. 'He needs you back,' David said. 'In fact, we all need you back to keep him happy.'

'It's nice to be wanted just for yourself.'

On the Friday he rang just as the group were saying goodbye, exchanging addresses and promising to keep in touch.

'I want a date,' he said. 'What are you doing on Sunday afternoon?'

'Nothing I can't put off. Why?'

'I'm in the flat. The things we bought have been arriving, and I've even got the boxes of my own stuff. I've got to make sense of everything. D'you fancy coming round and helping me? I need the suggestions of a home-maker.'

'A home-maker or a labourer?' she asked.

'Well, actually, a labourer. But I pay good rates. And I'll get you a banquet. A Chinese take-away.'

'I doubt a posh place like Ransome's Wharf will allow take-aways,' she said lightly, 'but I'll be happy to come and help.'

She was glad that she'd be seeing him so soon.

Next morning the drive over the Pennines was exhilarating. She didn't know why it should be, but the sun was out and the green mountains reminded her of what she was missing in her flat home territory. For some reason she felt better able to think about the letter from her parents. David had been right. After the passing of some time she was able to think about things without an automatic emotional response. She rehearsed the reasons for and against getting in touch with them as calmly and dispassionately as she could.

So far in her life she'd never worried about who her real parents were. She hadn't even wondered about them, even though she'd been told at an early age that she was adopted. Her life—with her mother and now with Peter—had been perfectly happy. Her real—if that was the right word—parents had given up their child. After twenty-nine years why should they want to reverse that decision?

But she knew, from working with the Samaritans, from listening to people revealing insoluble problems, that chance and circumstances could pile up against almost anyone. She recalled the number of sad stories she'd heard from people who'd done nothing wrong!

And didn't people change? Her parents were now nearly thirty years older.

She didn't need a new mother, new parents in her

life. Finding them might mean an emotional roller-coaster ride she was just not prepared for. But as she thought this, she knew what she was going to do. If nothing was ever risked, life would be very boring.

Of course, there was a middle course. She could write to them without revealing either her name or address, then if things didn't work out she could forget it. But as she thought this, she knew it wasn't true. Once contact had been made it would be almost impossible to back away.

As she dropped down onto the Lancashire plain she decided definitely that she would write. And she would do it at once.

She got home, shouted hello to Sue and Megan, took a cup of coffee up to her room and sat at her writing table. She took up her pen, wrote 'dear' and after five minutes put down her pen again. This was going to be hard. If she said how happy her childhood had been, would that be seen as a reproach to her biological mother? If she didn't, would that be an insult to the memory of her dead adopted mother?

Dear who? Mother, Ma, Mum? After ten minutes, staring at the one word, she scratched it out and wrote, 'I have just scratched out dear because I don't know what to call you. So I'll just tell you a bit about myself.' After that it got a bit easier. She didn't want to write too much, just a few facts. She mentioned her life, her training, the fact she was very happy as a nurse. She wasn't married, but one day she hoped to be. Then there was the difficult bit. She had to explain that she was doubtful about any meeting but that perhaps she was willing to try it. It was hard to explain because she wasn't really certain herself.

The letter was finished, reread and stuffed in an en-

velope. Then she hurried to the postbox, knowing that
if she held onto the letter she'd have second thoughts.
The second thoughts did come as she walked away—
but by then it was too late.

David's car drew up outside promptly at one the next
afternoon. Jane ran out to greet him, wearing the tracksuit she usually had on for slopping around the house.
In one bag she carried a selection of old clothes and in
another a selection of dusters, cleaning stuffs and pol-
ishes. She waved her bags at him. 'I'm coming to
work,' she said, 'and I'm dressed for it.'

He, too, was dressed for work. The muscles in his
thighs were outlined through his jeans, and the dusty T-
shirt he was wearing was far too tight. She hadn't seen
him for a week, and realised how much she'd missed
him. He kissed her. After a blissful minute she pushed
him away. 'Get in the car and drive,' she said. 'I'm in
the mood for work.'

'They've finished the place and cleaned it,' he said
as they travelled upwards in the lift at Ransome's Wharf
a little while later. 'I must say I'm very pleased. Or I
will be when I get all the stuff organised. You were
right about only getting the minimum at first—I
couldn't have coped with more. And I hadn't realised
how much stuff I'd acquired myself.'

First they went into the living room. The wooden
blinds had been fitted and looked well, the couch was
in position and the dull red material echoed the brick
walls perfectly. But in the middle of the room was a set
of teachests and carefully tied stout cardboard boxes.
'My life,' he said pointing at the boxes, 'all wrapped
up, ready to come out again.'

'Let's get started. I'll go and get changed.'

The first thing they did was find the box that held his music centre, for they'd already decided just where it was to go. Once that was out and installed he asked her to choose a CD. 'Music while we work,' he said.

She picked almost at random. There was a selection of songs from musical shows—that would do. Later, she promised herself, she would have a good look through the other titles. You could tell a lot about a man from his choice of music.

They opened more boxes. He started on his clothes while she sorted his books. Bookshelves had been delivered and fitted in the room that was to be his study, so she started to fill them.

They were interesting books. There were textbooks, of course, far more than he'd had in his hospital room. There was also a well-read set of Dickens, accounts of sea voyages and a surprising number of books on medicinal plants and herbs—including the famous Culpeper. 'Why so many books on herbs?' she shouted.

He poked his head round the study door. 'I think there's a lot of knowledge about herbal remedies that we ignore at our peril,' he said. 'Some research is now suggesting that some primitive peoples knew quite a bit.' He grinned. 'A pity they didn't know more about germs and so on.'

She picked up a large book, obviously expensive, of photographs of London. A well known photographer had taken them. 'This is nice,' she said, and opened the front cover. There she saw a vast dedication scrawled across a dark picture of London docks. It was in golden ink. 'To darling David. All my love and kisses, Diane.'

'This book is dedicated to you,' she said. '"All my love and kisses, Diane."'

He laughed. "'All my love and kisses'? I think that was a bit of an exaggeration.'

'But you've kept the book.'

'Because I like the pictures—no other reason.' He squinted at her. 'You almost sound jealous, Jane.'

'Don't be silly,' she snapped, and rapidly pushed books on the shelves to hide her confusion.

He walked away. The next big book she picked up intrigued her even more. It was a family photograph album. She couldn't help herself—she had to look inside. There were pictures of him as a schoolboy, as a young doctor, walking in the hills. She put it to one side as she wanted to go through it with him some time, and have him tell her all about each picture. She wanted to know him.

Next was a big folder marked 'Case Notes—David Kershaw'. This she didn't open. Instead, she carried it through to him. 'What's this, David?' she asked, though she thought she already knew.

His smile disappeared. 'I told you about my crash and the damage to my fingers.' He took the folder from her and leafed through it abstractedly. 'Perhaps it's not a good idea for a doctor to try to treat himself, but I wanted to make sure that everything possible had been done. These are my case notes. There are letters from no end of consultants, orthopaedic experts, neurologists, the lot. All of them say they can do so much—but never quite enough.'

She took the folder from him. 'No time to brood now. You've got work to do.'

Much of his personal belongings had been packed in a hurry so they needed pressing or washing or cleaning. She helped him to make piles and put the first ever load in the washing machine.

'You're to learn to operate this yourself,' she told him. 'I'll do it once for you. After that you're on your own.'

The crockery, cutlery, pots and pans had been delivered but not unpacked. The pile of paper and packaging grew steadily bigger, but the kitchen began to look as if someone lived there. She pulled the plastic covering off the newly delivered bed, and called David to help her make it with the new sheets. There was something peculiarly intimate about the operation and she bent her head so that he shouldn't see the slight redness in her face.

Finally it was time for him to take the boxes and the piles of packaging down to the basement. She dusted, brushed, vacuumed and cleared away the mess made by the unpacking. And then it was done. The flat still looked bare, but more like a home. There were pictures on the walls, a coffee-table for drinks and the couch to relax on. It looked good.

She felt warm, with a sense of satisfaction. Checking her watch, she saw that they had worked non-stop for nearly five hours. When David came back he put a friendly arm round her shoulders. 'Go and have a bath,' he said. 'I promised you a banquet—I'll go to fetch it.'

'What about you? Surely you're tired, too?' He looked weary, but happy. There were dark stains under his armpits and smudges on his face.

'I'm all right for the moment. I'll have a bath when I come back. Then we can both relax.'

She filled the bath and got undressed. She heard him shout, 'Back on ten minutes.' Then the door slammed. She prepared to get into the bath—and suddenly roared with rueful laughter. It was a good thing that he didn't hear her.

*   *   *

'It's a bit chilly, but why don't you sit on the balcony and relax for a while?' David said. 'Put my coat round you and have a glass of wine. It's very pleasant out there.'

'Sounds like a good idea,' Jane said demurely, and followed his suggestion.

He had returned with a variety of cartons and had slipped them into the oven to reheat. She realised that a take-away it might be, but it was a superior one. He'd opened a bottle of wine and he poured her a glass, taking his own away with him. She sat, sipping her wine and watching the lights on the river. It was romantic. Very. She laughed again.

Behind her she heard him setting the table in the dining section in the kitchen, putting out the new cutlery and crockery. Then there was a silence, and in the distance she heard the drumming sound of water being poured into the bath. This was a super red wine, obviously very expensive. She sipped, and laughed again.

He reappeared a little later, hair slicked back and dressed in dark blue jeans and shirt. 'Dinner is served, madam,' he said. She followed him back to the kitchen.

He had put more music on, a CD of some piano music, distant and dreamy. The meal was indeed a banquet, but she had worked hard so she felt entitled to enjoy her food. He poured more wine. Afterwards they went back into the living room and he dragged the couch to where they could sit and look at the river, before bringing a filled coffee-pot. There were also two small glasses, into which he poured a dark green liqueur. 'Benedictine,' he told her, 'from my last trip abroad. I was saving it for an occasion like this.'

They drank the liqueur and coffee. He put his arm round her shoulders and she leaned against him. She felt warm and happy, but mischief welled up inside her. Suddenly she couldn't contain herself any longer. She laughed.

It surprised him, even shocked him. 'What's so funny?' he asked uncertainly.

She giggled again. 'I don't know that it's funny. In fact, it's half tragic. I feel terrible really. Because I know what you're doing now. The meal, the drink—you want me to stay the night, don't you?'

'The thought had crossed my mind,' he said cautiously, 'but, of course, it's entirely up to you.'

'I would like to,' she told him. 'I would like to in every possible way. But every way just isn't possible. David, because of an unavoidable and specifically female condition which has just started—a little early, in fact—all we could do is sleep. Tonight, or in the next three or four nights.'

She looked at him and collapsed, giggling, again. 'Oh, David, if you could just see your face! Come on, you obviously know about these problems.'

'I'm a doctor, of course I do! It's just that...' Reluctantly, he, too, saw the funny side. 'I suppose you can't win them all,' he said. 'That's the truest saying I know. Come on, more coffee?'

She leaned over to kiss him. 'You're a wonderful, wonderful man,' she said. 'Yes, I'll have more coffee.'

Later he offered to run her home, or said she could stay if she wanted. She did want to stay in that new bed they'd just made, but she thought the frustration would be too much. For her as well as for him. 'Take me home,' she said. 'It's such a pity, David.'

CHAPTER SIX

THERE were the usual pre-operation chores for Jane in the morning. First, a quick glance at the list pinned by the changing room door. Nothing out of the way. Then into the anteroom to greet Mary Barnes who was now her runner. After her shaky start she had become the perfect Theatre assistant. While Jane stood by her trolley, handing things to the surgeon, Mary fetched anything extra Mr Steadman might need. She was an extra pair of hands for Jane—and often they were needed. When Mr Steadman needed something in Theatre, he needed it *now*.

'You're looking cheerful this morning,' Mary said. 'Have a good weekend?' She finished scrubbing up, having taken the statutory three minutes.

'It had its moments,' Jane said ruefully. 'Trolley ready?'

'Already covered in its green cloth. But I'll go through and check everything.' Mary walked through to the instrument room.

Jane rubbed the pink antiseptic soap into her hands and started to scrub up herself. 'Morning, David.' She was rinsing her arms as he came into the anteroom so there was no way she could do more than twist round and smile at him.

He had a paper in his hand which seemed to greatly interest him because he didn't reply. Perhaps he hadn't heard.

'I had a super surprise last night,' she said smilingly. 'I was—'

'I'm sure you did. Now, could we keep the social chit-chat till a more appropriate time? We have work to do here.'

She looked at him, astounded. Had he really spoken to her like that? His face was remote, his voice curt and chill. She said, 'David, I...' But he had left the room.

In Theatre he kept his head down, and there were no remarks to her and Edmund when things were going well. Even Edmund noticed it. 'Everything all right, David?'

'Just keeping my eye on this gauge, Edmund. I'm a tiny touch concerned about the heartbeat. Nothing for you to worry about.'

'Let me know if there is.' Edmund bent to his task. He had one job, his anaesthetist another.

At lunchtime David hurried off, and he didn't join Jane in the canteen. Perhaps there was something wrong, but she hoped not.

She managed to speak to him before the afternoon list started. 'David, is there anything wrong? You seem to be—'

'There's nothing whatsoever wrong with me. Thank you for your concern, but I really don't need it.' And he brushed past her. She stared after him, open-mouthed.

That night, between choir practice and doing her washing, she tried to phone him three times. Each time she reached his answerphone and asked him to ring her back. He didn't bother. First she was concerned, then she was upset, finally she got angry. No one treated her this way.

He was as cold as ever next morning, but she paid

no attention to him. However, at the end of the morning's list she managed to get him on his own in the anteroom. 'David, could we have a word?'

'I'm afraid I don't have time right now.' He tried to get by her, but she moved quickly, put her hand on his chest and pushed him back.

'David, you owe me an explanation. If you don't want to see me any more, that's fine. But I would appreciate a little courtesy. Just one sentence would have done. I don't mind being insulted, but I won't be ignored. Now, just tell me we're…finished and, if you can, why. Then I'll never bother you again.'

'I'll give you just one sentence,' he said savagely. 'Or perhaps two or three. I had an early call yesterday morning. Like a love-struck teenager, I drove past your house. I looked at your bedroom window and there was a man, in pyjamas, looking out. He was yawning—he'd obviously spent the night there. Then I saw you in your dressing-gown behind him. You hugged him. I hope he was worth it.'

She looked at him, white-faced, unable to speak. When he tried to move past her she said, 'Now it's my turn for one sentence, if not two or three. Yes, he spent the night on Sunday, and d'you know what? He gave me some money. Makes it even worse, doesn't it? He's younger than you, David, not quite as good-looking but very presentable. I had a wonderful evening with him. He's got an awful lot of qualities that you don't have, that you'll never have.'

Now he, too, was white-faced. 'I don't care to hear any more,' he said.

'Well, unfortunately, you're going to have to. You've missed the best part. He did sleep in my bedroom, but he slept on the floor. He's done it quite often before. I didn't tell you his name, did I? It's Peter Cabot. He's my brother. I've been supporting him through medical school. Now he's a house officer and he's getting paid at last so he wants to start paying me back. That's the money. We don't usually allow men to stay overnight in the house, we have rules against it, but brothers are an exception. Happy now, David?

She had seen the comprehension slowly dawning on his face. He believed her, of course. Why shouldn't he. It was the truth.

His voice was anguished. 'Jane…Jane, what can I say?'

'You can't say anything. You've already said it. I think it's a joke, coming from you, feeling entitled to suspect other people. You, the world's greatest multiple lover. It's a question of trust, David. You didn't ask, you didn't give me the chance to explain—you just made up your mind. I'm still not sure whether to trust you or not. But, whatever you did, I would always have asked you if you had anything to say.'

'Jane, I—'

'I haven't finished. Don't try to explain, don't be sorry. It's too late. We'll work together, be pleasant to each other, we're part of a team. But anything else between us is finished. Now you can work your way through all the Sister Fallows of the hospital. And good luck to you.'

She brushed past him, but he turned and reached out to catch her arm. She stopped and brushed off his hand. 'Don't come after me,' she said, the calmness of her voice not masking the ferocity behind it. 'Everything has already been said.' When she set off again he didn't follow her.

She had enjoyed making her little speech, it had satisfied her. Her anger had been genuine and she had meant every word. But when she got to the front door of her house that night she felt less happy. Now that the rage had gone, there was a deep sadness. She had liked David so much, they had such a lot in common. In fact, she was in… She couldn't bring herself even to think the word.

And she had to keep up the appearance of cheerfulness for Peter. He had come up late on Sunday, the first break he'd had from his arduous house officer's job. And he was loving the work.

He'd brought her money and had said it was the first instalment of what he owed her. She'd tried to refuse it because she'd happily paid for his training.

'I have my pride, you know,' he'd said threateningly. 'We agreed when I took the money that I could pay it back.'

'And I have my pride, too,' she'd replied. Then they'd both giggled, and she'd said, 'Tell you what, we'll split the difference. I'll take half. And when you're a consultant you can give me the balance then.'

Sue and Megan had insisted that the rules against men staying over didn't apply to brothers and sisters, so Peter was staying in her room. It was like old times again.

He had been tall and gangling, even at eighteen, but since then he'd filled out. Hard work and exercise had made him much more solid. The child's face had become more serious and he looked like a good doctor. But when he smiled she still remembered the little lad whose swing she'd pushed when they were young, and the walks they'd had, hand in hand, through the park.

'Smells good,' she said as she walked into the kitchen. He stood up from the oven and grinned.

'I'm a well-brought-up young man,' he said. 'Someone taught me how to cook when I was young. Like my pinny?'

Over his jeans and shirt he was wearing an apron he must have found in one of the kitchen drawers. It was floral, and far too small for him. She laughed. 'Just don't let any of your patients see you dressed like that.'

'I certainly won't. When I got my long white coat I practised the cool, assessing medical look. It's a strain on the face, but it works.' He reached for the kettle. 'Cup of tea?'

'Love one. And what's that cooking? I'm ravenous.' Because of her argument with David she hadn't wanted to eat in the canteen—her anger had kept her going. But now she was hungry.

'Ah. What's cooking is chilli con carne, very nourishing and tasty, too. But all the experts agree that it's better cooked and then left to rest for a day, so we'll have it tomorrow. I've even cooked extra so you can freeze some.'

He'd turned his back to her to make the tea. But he was her little brother and she *knew* him.

'Come on, Peter. First of all, I'm hungry now. I don't want to wait till tomorrow to eat. Secondly, you're hiding something. Out with it!'

'So much for doctors not letting their emotions show,' he muttered. 'It's all a bit complicated. The fact is, sister, I got a phone call this afternoon. I've been invited out to dinner. You're invited, too, if you want to come. And I think I'd like you to come.'

She sat at the kitchen table and remained silent till he was seated opposite her and had pushed a mug of tea across to her. 'Who's invited you out to dinner? And me as well if I want to come?' Her voice was dangerously calm.

He came round the table and put his arm round her shoulders. For a moment she resisted, then she leaned against him. He was bigger than she was. For years, when he'd been a boy and so much smaller than her, he had leaned against her in just this way. Now things had changed, and he was a man. And now she found she liked leaning against him.

'You know very well who's invited us out to dinner. David Kershaw. He said he wanted to take me out to dinner because he owed me an apology. He told me about seeing me in pyjamas at your window, and what he'd thought. He said the least he could do was feed me. But we don't have to go if you don't want. I said I'd ring to confirm things. He said he felt wrecked, and he sounded it, too.'

'Good,' said Jane. 'I hope he's suffering.' This was the last thing she'd expected. How did she feel? What she'd said to David had been final and definitive, and she'd meant it. Their affair was over. But now he was trying to make amends. Did she want him back? The raw anger was still there, but there was another emotion she could feel. She felt relief. She wanted him back.

Peter was looking at her anxiously. 'You haven't mentioned this fellow in your letters, Jane. Just how serious are things?'

'Probably more serious than they should be. I went out with him to start with on a very casual basis. He doesn't seem a very good investment, Peter.'

'Well, I liked the sound of him. We had a long talk about medicine, and there's a couple of things he could tell me. Did you know he started off wanting to be a surgeon?'

'Yes, I knew. I know a lot about him.'

'Anyway…' Her brother's arm was still round her, and she was still leaning on him. It was comforting. 'He sent you a message, via me. A bit of a peculiar one, really. I've never had to pass on anything like this before. He said he's never said it to you directly—but he loves you.'

'He does what? He loves me? I must say, he has a funny way of showing it.'

Peter squeezed her. 'You've usually had good taste in men, Jane. I liked John Gilmore. Are you going to give this David Kershaw a chance? It's your decision. If not, I'll phone him and we'll eat chilli con carne.'

'I suppose we'd better go,' she said wearily. 'You'd better phone him to make arrangements. Say we'll come out with him if you can drive his car.'

'What sort of a car has he got?'

'It's a Porsche. It's his pet.'

'A Porsche!' Peter may have been a doctor, but there was still something of the little boy in him. 'I wonder if he will let me have a drive?' Then he sighed. 'No need even to think about it. I won't be insured. What colour is it, Jane? How old is it?'

'He'll tell you all that, and you can talk about your Dinky collections. Just phone him and tell him he can take us somewhere expensive.'

'I think he'd already decided that.' Peter kissed her on the cheek 'All right, little sister?'

'Yes. I'm all right. Tell him he can take us to dinner. And tell him that this doesn't mean that he's forgiven. It's dinner only.'

'I think he knows that.'

Peter phoned, and arranged that they would be picked up at eight. 'We're going to Chez Picard,' he said. 'What's that like?'

Jane winced. 'That *is* expensive,' she said. 'You're not allowed in the car park with anything less than a Jaguar. I hope he doesn't think he can buy me.'

'He can buy me,' Peter said. 'Well, he can buy me a meal. Now, shall I do you a quick cheese sandwich to keep you going?'

Peter went to change first and came down looking very much the young doctor in a dark suit, white shirt and college tie. 'Very professional,' she said. 'Now it's my turn.'

Megan had arrived home by the time she came back down, and was having an earnest conversation at the kitchen table with Peter. The two had much in common. They looked up.

'Jane, you look gorgeous,' Megan gasped.

She had let down her hair, brushed and tied it back. She wore a little more make-up than usual, with a touch of perfume. She was wearing a minidress in grey silk, sleeveless and showing much leg. It wasn't quite the thing for getting in and out of a sports car, but for once she didn't mind.

Peter smiled proudly. He knew his sister well. 'You want to make him suffer, don't you?' he said. 'Well, you will, wearing that dress.'

'Let him know what he's missing,' said Jane.

David knocked on the door at two minutes to eight, and Peter let him in. For Jane there was a bunch of red and cream roses, and she read the card that came with them. It simply said, 'Sorry.' He looked at her with a small smile.

'They're really nice,' she said unenthusiastically. 'I'll

put them in some water.' She knew what she was doing to him, and she didn't mind at all!

With difficulty the three of them managed to fit into the Porsche. She insisted on going in the back—after all, she had the shortest legs. Perhaps wisely, David concentrated on talking to Peter, and Jane was glad of this. It gave the two a chance to get to know each other, and she still wasn't sure about her feelings for David. Fortunately, Peter and David had a lot in common. They prattled on about medicine and cars, and after a while she felt almost left out of the conversation.

The meal at Chez Picard was superb. They sat in a banquette, enjoying course after delicious course. She chose a starter of chicken poached in a white wine sauce, with rocket and fennel leaves. Then there was turbot, with a vast selection of vegetables, and, to finish, ice cream in a spun sugar basket. She was a good eater and she thoroughly enjoyed it all.

David still didn't say very much to her, continuing to be in deep conversation with Peter. He treated her as a colleague and friend, not as a lover. She thought this showed a certain delicacy on his part, that he didn't think that everything was back to normal. But she had to admit to herself that she felt better towards him by the end of the meal. Food always makes me happy, she thought with amusement.

They had coffee and David drove them home. With some tact, Peter said goodbye to David and walked to the front door, leaving David to help Jane out of the back of the Porsche. Her skirt rode up—as she had known it would—and he glanced expressionlessly from the long length of her leg to her eyes. He, too, knew why she had worn that particular dress.

'I've enjoyed this evening—I think,' he said. 'I like your brother, he's good company.'

'I've also enjoyed the evening—I think,' she replied. 'Thank you for a very pleasant meal.'

He winced a bit at her false politeness, but said nothing about it. 'Will I see you tomorrow?'

'Of course—we're working together.'

'That's not exactly what I meant. Will *I* be seeing *you*?'

'It's going to take time, David,' she told him, 'but I think we'll be friends again soon.'

'That's fair enough. I could apologise again, but I doubt if it would do any good. You already know how I feel about you, don't you?'

She was silent for a moment. 'You told Peter to tell me that you loved me. Why was that?'

He, too, was silent, then he said, 'You may not believe this, but the only other woman I have ever said I loved was…was Diane. I've never said it to anyone else.'

'So we're not just having a casual affair? This is serious, is it? David, what if I *want* it just to be casual?'

He sighed. 'It's your decision, of course. But I'm hoping that in time you'll get to…care for me as much as I care for you. Come on, you'll be getting cold like that. You'd better get inside.'

He walked her to the open front door and said, 'Goodnight, Jane.' Then he turned and was gone. He had made no attempt to kiss her. Good. She heard the rumble of the engine, and watched the car move away.

'Well, I liked him, Jane,' Peter said later as they sat at the kitchen table. 'Obviously I won't interfere, but are you going to forgive him?'

'I'm thinking about it. Trust is very important to me, and for a while there he didn't trust me.'

'He will next time. If I were you, I'd give him another chance.'

It wasn't the same as it had been in Theatre for the next day or two. David obviously knew that he wasn't to presume for he smiled gingerly and she was professional without being too friendly. But they were still part of a good team.

'I liked your brother,' he'd said when they'd had a moment together on Wednesday. 'He's got all the makings of a good doctor. He asked interesting questions.'

'He liked you, too,' she'd told him, 'but that might just be a sign that the Cabots are bad at judging people.'

He'd sighed. 'I suppose I deserved that. Are you still hurting, Jane?'

She'd thought about the question for a moment. 'Yes,' she'd said, 'I'm still hurting. I might be able to understand, but I feel betrayed.'

'That makes me feel worse than ever, but I hope that in time you'll—'

Then, as so often happened, they'd been interrupted. The anteroom of an operating Theatre was no place to conduct a long personal conversation.

When she got home on Friday there was a letter waiting for her. She knew who it was from at once. She wanted to put off reading it till, say, later in the evening. She might feel more…confident then. Her emotions were already in a turmoil. But there was choir practice later, and she wasn't going to miss it.

The postmark showed that the letter came from a small town in Yorkshire just over the Pennines. She felt more uneasy than ever. Recently she'd had one emotional upset and she wasn't in the mood for another. Should she put the letter in the drawer and wait until she felt calmer? No. She'd started this so she'd carry on.

The letter was written on headed notepaper. There was also an e-mail address. That made things worse. These were real people, with a real address and real feelings. If she read on she knew she'd have to worry and wonder about what they thought. She read on.

Dear Jane,

I'm not exactly writing back at once. In fact, I've had parts of this letter ready for weeks. I know what I want to say—or I think I do. I wrote to the society, and hoped that you would get in touch. Then it was so good to get your letter. You seem to be a success, happy in your work and I trust you will decide to marry in time. There are many questions I want to ask you, but I'd really like to ask you in person—if you want that, too.

There are things I want you to know. This is not an excuse, but an explanation. I want you to know how it came about that I offered you for adoption. If you only knew how much the decision hurt me.

Nearly thirty years ago, when I was eighteen, I became pregnant. I was a student in a teacher training college, intending to teach primary school children. I wanted to do so much, I was so enjoying the course. My boyfriend at the time was Colin. He was a year older than me, and had just gone to Africa for a year to work in a school out there. We were serious about each other, but I knew this trip was what he wanted and I couldn't stand in his way, even though I knew I'd miss him.

It was a fortnight after he'd left that I found I was pregnant. There was no way I could get in touch with him—he had gone upcountry. My parents were dead. I had been brought up by an aunt and I knew she wouldn't be very sympathetic. I perhaps could have had an abortion. It was my own decision that I didn't want this. So I had you, and I was persuaded that the best thing to do was offer you for adoption. You must remember that things were very different thirty years ago, women having babies and careers wasn't half as common as it is now.

I didn't tell Colin what had happened when he came back. We got married, and after two or three years I did tell him. He was terribly upset. He wanted to get in touch with you at once, said we ought at least to find out if you were all right, but I thought it in your best interests not to do anything. So, reluctantly, he agreed with me.

We have been married twenty-five years now. He's a primary school headmaster, and I teach part time after I brought up the children. We had two more children—Maria, who is eighteen, and Mark, who is twenty-one. They might look like you as they are your brother and sister.

I would like to meet you, perhaps, if that's the way it goes, only once. But I would like to meet you. I've thought about it so often, and didn't write, partly out of cowardice, partly because I thought it might upset you. But I'd like to meet you now. If you don't want to meet, then I fully understand, you have a good life of your own. I know I have no call on you.

I hope you don't mind if I finish this letter—Love, Marion Stott.

Underneath was a line in a different hand. 'And I want so much to meet you too. God Bless You, Colin Stott.'

She read through the letter four times, not knowing what to make of the chaotic emotions she was feeling. One thing she did know—it had upset her. She'd thought she'd had her emotions, her attitude to her family, well under control. She'd been so happy at home that she'd never even thought about the woman who'd given her up. It had been none of her business. And now, suddenly, it was her business. She wasn't sure she liked it. First the trouble with David, now this. How was she going to cope?

But life had to go on. It was choir practice tonight, and she had to go to that. She went to get changed.

For all the good she did, she might as well have stayed at home. At long last the choir had got things right, and they were singing like professionals. All on her own, Jane dragged them back to sounding like amateurs again.

She'd also intended to do a session with the Samaritans that night. Wisely, she phoned to cancel. She was aware that she'd be unable to concentrate on other people's emotional problems, and was likely to have done more harm than good.

'Would you like me to arrange some counselling?' her leader asked her.

'No, thanks. I can sort things out myself,' she said. Even as she spoke the words, she knew she was wrong. She needed to talk to someone.

Saturday was little better. She played hockey as if she were dreaming, fouling people, missing passes, being in the wrong place. She couldn't concentrate. What made things worse was that everyone forgave her. 'We all have bad days,' the captain said good-naturedly. Jane felt she would rather have been shouted at.

By Sunday morning she realised that things couldn't go on like this any longer. She was still walking around in a dream—cleaning her teeth twice in a row, forgetting to put the tea in the teapot, narrowly avoiding an accident as she turned into the drive of the house. Next day was Monday, when she had to be a scrub nurse again. No way could she avoid being alert for that.

She needed to talk to someone. Megan and Sue were the two obvious choices, but they both knew her too well to give her the detached advice she needed. Detached—that was the operative word. She needed someone detached. Who was the expert she knew on keeping emotions at bay? Not that he'd been doing too well recently. She phoned David on his mobile.

'I need advice,' she said abruptly. 'Nothing to do with you and me, it's just about me. I want someone detached to tell me what to do.'

'I'm not detached from you, Jane—at least, I don't want to be. But I'm happy to help you if I can. Shall I come to your house or will you come to my flat?'

Already, the sound of that calm voice was persuading her that there would be some kind of answer to her problems, but she didn't fancy either of the two alternatives he'd suggested.

'Neither. I want to meet you on some kind of… neutral ground. You come in your car, I'll come in mine.'

'As you wish. But it's a bit cold for meeting outside.'

She paused. 'There's a pub called the Old Ferry, where they used to row people across the river. It's down a little road from Wenton. You park this side of the railway line and walk over.'

'I've never been there but I know where you mean and I'll find it. When shall I see you?'

She glanced at the clock on the wall. Twenty past eleven. 'In about an hour? At half past twelve?'

'I'll see you there.'

Before he could ring off she said, 'And remember, David, this is not about us. I've got other things on my mind.'

'That's fair enough. But I'm glad you feel you can call on me. Half past twelve, then.' He rang off.

It was much colder now. There was no sun and the wind was chilly. Winter was arriving. She dragged out her duffle-coat and put it on over her sweater and trousers, then drove to the Old Ferry.

There weren't as many cars as there were in summer, but the Porsche was already there. David was always punctual. She climbed the bridge over the railway line, and stopped to look at the vast width of the river and the thin line of hills on the other side. The view made her problems seem less important, more capable of solution. She would work something out.

There were wooden benches outside the pub, but it was cold and only one man was sitting there. It was David, wearing a thick climber's anorak over cords and a sweater. When he saw her approaching he stood and smiled tentatively.

'I thought it a bit early for alcohol, so I ordered a tray of sandwiches and some coffee. But I'll get you some wine if you like.'

She shook her head. 'Coffee is fine. Can we stay out here? That coat of yours looks warm enough.'

'It is. And we can stay where you like. Has Peter gone back?'

'He's back in London. He wants me to go down to visit him soon.'

David nodded but said nothing. Someone must have been watching them, for a girl brought out sandwiches and a pot of coffee. David poured for them, and she wrapped her fingers round the warm mug.

'I like looking at the view here,' he said. 'It's so tranquil. So I'll sit and watch, and you start when you're ready.'

She shouldn't have forgotten how responsive to her moods he was. Somehow he knew that she wanted a few minutes' silence before she could talk.

Together they stared at the mudbanks and the polished silver surface of the river, marked only by the odd ripple where the wind brushed it. Only a week ago she would have reached out and held his hand. She didn't now. Perhaps, later on, she might.

It was time to talk. 'I told you I was adopted, that my real mother—that is, my birth mother—wrote to me about wanting to meet. You told me there was no hurry, to wait till I knew what I wanted. Well, I wrote to her. And she wrote back at once. It's thrown me and I don't know what to think or do. This is it.'

She handed him the letter. He read it through twice carefully, then slipped it back in the envelope. 'What do you think you think?' he asked. 'If that sentence makes sense.'

'I'm confused. I've got one family, even though it's just Peter. I'm not sure that I want another.'

'Are you worried about what Peter would feel? Because I'll say straight away that although I've only met him once he struck me as a very well-balanced young man. I don't think he'd have any problem coping with you getting an extra relation or two.'

'I suppose you're right. The thing is, if I go any further—if I meet them—then they'll be mine. There's no way I can ever forget them again. And that frightens me. I think I wish I hadn't written.'

'It would frighten me, too.' He pushed the sandwiches towards her. 'Eat, and keep up the blood sugar.' After a pause he said, 'This is to do with your character. You never back away from a fight, a confrontation.' He smiled ironically, 'I know that if anyone does. Jane, do you think you'll ever be happy if you don't go to see them?'

She bit into a ham sandwich. 'No,' she said. 'When it comes down to it, I know I've got to see them.'

He frowned and picked up the letter again. After re-reading it, he said, 'I might be wrong, I might be completely wrong. And I'm not sure you'll want to hear what I have to say because it'll influence you. But I think there's something you've missed in this letter.'

'Missed something! The number of times I've read it?'

'Perhaps you're too close.'

'Don't be irritating,' she snapped. 'I've read it every half-hour for the past two days. I've missed nothing.'

'Perhaps not. Why have they waited so long to get in touch? She acknowledges that it might have been kinder not to do so. What about that one-line message to you from Colin. ''I want so much to meet you, too''?'

'Well, what about it? You tell me. I did wonder about it.'

Choosing his words carefully, David said, 'I wonder if perhaps one of them might be seriously—dangerously—ill. A case of putting their life in order before it's too late.'

'Give me that letter!' She read through it, even though she now practically knew its contents by heart.

Yes, now she could see what David meant. 'For a primary school headmaster, his handwriting is a bit erratic,' she said.

'As if he was having difficulty holding the pen.'

She looked at David with gloomy respect. This was just the kind of subtle idea she might have expected from him. 'I think you might be right,' she said. 'So now what do I do?'

He pointed to her plate. 'Forget things for a moment. Finish your sandwich, and have another one. You'll feel better then. Look, there's a great flock of geese overhead. Going to Canada or somewhere.'

She looked upwards at a great arrowhead of birds, flying towards the sea. Distantly they heard a hoarse honking sound.

'Wish I were a bird,' she said. 'Just flying here, there and everywhere, honking at people and being ignored.'

'They have their problems, too. If you were a lady goose you'd have to find somewhere to lay your eggs, somewhere where people like me couldn't get at them. I'm very fond of a boiled goose egg.'

She giggled. 'Just think, me and geese having exactly the same low opinion of you. Makes me feel I'm not alone. These sandwiches are very nice.'

They finished the sandwiches, and he poured her another coffee. Then she said, 'Yes, I do feel better. And I know what I'm going to do. I'm going to see them, aren't I?'

'I would say that you are. You'll never be content till you have. And what's more, you'll want to do it quickly. What about next weekend?'

Her first reaction was to say no at once. But he was

right. This was something she had to do quickly. 'I suppose it's possible,' she said. 'Or perhaps the weekend after if—'

'Do it soon. In fact, do it now. I've got a suggestion. There's an e-mail address here. I've just been connected to the Internet, so why not come back to my flat and send a message at once? It's more impersonal than phoning, but a lot quicker than ordinary mail. And if you don't ever want to see them again, then I'm a dead end. They can't get my address from an e-mail.'

She looked at him suspiciously. 'You're taking a big interest in my affairs,' she said.

'And I want to take an even bigger interest. I suggest I drive you over if they can see you next weekend. I could drop you there and wander round for a couple of hours while you get acquainted. It might not be a good idea for you to drive yourself. You might be a bit…fraught when you've been there.'

She sat, thinking. She knew that her life would be easier once she'd made a decision. It was the uncertainty that distracted her. And she wanted to see her real parents—especially if one of them was ill.

'All right. Let's e-mail them,' she said. 'What's in this for you, David?'

'I'm hoping to be forgiven in time,' he said flatly, 'but I don't expect it to be quite yet.'

She followed his car back to his flat, then sat in front of the monitor in the little room he now used as a study. She had used e-mail at work, but they weren't connected at home. At work there seemed to be as many jokes being transmitted as there were serious messages. 'What should I say?' she asked.

'Be simple, short and direct. Say you've received the letter and why not just ask if you could call for a couple of hours next Saturday or Sunday? Say at one o'clock. Keep any emotion for the meeting.'

'Keep any emotion for the meeting,' she repeated. 'All right, I'll start now.'

She'd used a keyboard often before, even if in a very amateurish way, but now she couldn't make her fingers touch the keys. He realised what was wrong so he leaned over her and typed for her.

'Thanks for your letter. If it's convenient, could I call to see you for a couple of hours, say at about one next Saturday or Sunday? Otherwise, what time would suit you best?'

She knew he was looking down at her, but she didn't lift her head from the keyboard. 'Will that do?' he asked.

'That's fine. Short and unemotional, as you suggested.'

'So how do I sign it? Regards? Sincerely? Love?'

'I've not had any success with love recently. Just sign it Jane.'

He did as she'd asked, then transmitted the message. They watched and saw that the message had got through, then David went off-line. 'Most people check their e-mail once a day,' he said, 'sometimes more often. I'll let you know when there's a reply.'

'Thanks,' she said dully. It was only the middle of the day, but already she felt lethargic. All this emotion was tiring!

'What are you going to do now?'

She shrugged. 'Nothing much. Please, don't invite me out anywhere. I'm not fit company for anyone.'

'I can't spare the time to take you out, Jane.' He gestured to the computer. 'There's a great amount of stuff I've got to get up to date, results to collate, articles to check over. I'm going to be busy on the computer all afternoon. But if you want to drag the couch in front of the window and watch the shipping go by, you're very welcome. It's hypnotic, very soothing. I do it a lot.'

'All right,' she said, 'but we're not to disturb each other.'

He was right, the slowly changing river scene was hypnotic. For a while she wanted to do nothing but not think. And it worked. After a while she closed her eyes, just for a moment.

When she opened them again it was getting dark. 'Have I slept all this time?' she asked fretfully.

'You were tired. Sleep is the body's natural way of coping with stress. Would you like me to make you something to eat?'

She struggled to her feet, stretched and yawned. 'No, thank you, David. Just a coffee or something and then I'll drive back. I need to be at home.'

He didn't press her. After she'd drunk her coffee he took her down to her car. She opened the door, turned and kissed him on the cheek. 'Thank you, David, you've been a big help.'

He was still standing there as she drove away.

When she arrived home Sue said, 'David rang. Will you ring him back at once?' She went on, 'Are things better between you now?'

'Well, they're improving,' Jane said thoughtfully. 'We'll just have to see how they go.'

She rang David's number. 'There's an e-mail message for you,' David said. 'It reads, "Either day fine, but hope to see you at one on Saturday. Looking forward so much to seeing you. I'm a bit frightened.

Love.'' And there a road map of the town, showing where their street is.'

'She's feeling the same as I am,' Jane said. 'A bit frightened. I wonder if this is going to be a success.'

'I would have thought it will be. See you tomorrow, but I'll pick you up at about nine next Saturday?'

'Fine,' she said.

CHAPTER SEVEN

USING sodium valproate had done little to help Mrs Todd's post-herpetic neuralgia. In fact, it had made her feel sick, so David was going to try acupuncture. They walked to the ward together.

'This technique was first described in a book published two thousand four hundred years ago,' he told Jane. 'It was called *The Yellow Emperor's Classic of Internal Medicine*.'

'That doesn't fill me with confidence. I'd be happier with sodium valproate. I can understand that. But are you happy with all this talk of yin and yang and chi and meridians?'

'Ah, I see you have been doing some research. The honest answer is that now there's a lot of scientifically provable truth in the old ideas. We can find the so-called trigger points with a sensitive electronic device. There's less electrical resistance than other parts of the body. Acupuncture works, Jane, and if we don't yet know why, we're at least learning.'

Mrs Todd was as stoic as ever, and quite interested in the new technique. 'One of my neighbours had it, Doctor, when she was having a baby. Worked a treat for her, it did. No pain at all. I thought that wasn't natural.'

'Who was this?' Jane asked, interested.

'It was young Eileen Tong. She runs a fish and chip shop.'

Oriental therapy or not, David was still observing

Western antiseptic precautions. He drew on gloves and then Jane handed him a sterile pack of the fine stainless-steel needles. They were 'sharps', and afterwards would be disposed of in the special container.

She was fascinated as he carefully chose his place, inserted the needle and then twisted it between his thumb and finger. 'Can you feel anything, Mrs Todd?'

'Well, it doesn't hurt. Tingles a bit, in fact.'

David had inserted the first needle high into Mrs Todd's chest. Jane tried desperately to remember her anatomy. Surely there was no nerve there that had anything to do with the pain that Mrs Todd suffered. The next four needles seemed to be inserted into equally pointless places.

'You know about endorphins?' he asked her as they walked away half an hour later.

'Yes. They're pain-relieving chemicals released by the brain.'

'Well, there's some suggestion that acupuncture stimulates their release. Exactly how we'll find out in time. But for the moment Mrs Todd will benefit anyway.'

The rest of the week took a lot out of Jane. They were as busy as ever in Theatre, with one or two extra-long operations. She saw a lot of David, but necessarily in the company of other people. They were now more friendly, if not yet quite back to their original state.

There were two rehearsals of the choir, and she was co-opted into doing an extra session for the Samaritans because two people were off sick. She enjoyed these activities as they took her mind away from her own problems.

'I've hardly seen you all week,' David said on Friday.

'Just one of those things,' she told him. 'I'm not avoiding you.'

'You're not seeking me out either.'

'True. I'm doing what is usually called keeping my head down. I just want to get tomorrow over with, and then I'll be able to see how things are going.'

'I sympathise, I really do. And I'll have your company for quite a few hours tomorrow, won't I?'

'Don't count on it being an enjoyable experience. I think I'm going to be a very scratchy person travelling there. And I've no idea how I'll be when we come back.'

She sat on her bed later that night, trying to decide what to wear. In all the women's magazines she had ever read there had never been an article on what to wear when meeting your mother for the first time in thirty years. She had to be comfortable but she had to look smart, though not excessively so. In the end she chose a light blue trouser suit and a darker blue sweater that complemented her eyes. They would have to do.

When David called next morning, he was wearing a sports jacket with a dark shirt and tie. He looked fine, neither too formal nor too casual. 'I was wondering all evening what I should wear,' she told him.

'This is your mother you're going to meet. It's not your clothes that will interest her. She'll look at your face, and be pleased that she's got a beautiful daughter.'

'David Kershaw! If I didn't know you better I'd say that speech had been rehearsed.'

'It wasn't rehearsed. It came from the heart.'

'Well, it was a lovely compliment. Now, let's get on the road.'

They set off for the M62. The little spurt of pleasure he had brought her soon evaporated, and she started to worry. The two of them had been getting on better, talking more, but once in the car she found she had nothing to say. He recognised her mood and put soft music on the radio. It helped her a little.

She didn't know what to expect of this visit, and thought that there was no longer any point in going over it with David. But what else could she do? After an hour she turned to him in desperation and said, 'I get there, the door opens and what do I say? Hello, I'm your long lost daughter? Or, nice to meet you, Mrs Stott? What happens if they don't like me?'

'You're panicking,' he said quietly, 'which is understandable and quite comforting. Any girl who wasn't worried in this situation wouldn't be normal. Don't plan anything. Remember, they're probably far more afraid than you are. You're a nice person—just be yourself.'

'But what if I come over all hard and cold? I don't want that.'

'You won't, you just won't,' he reassured her.

They drove in silence for another fifteen minutes, then Jane said, 'I know you get on with your parents, you love them. What would it be like if you found you had another set? How would you feel?'

'I'd be terrified. And amazed. Apparently, I look so much like my father when he was my age that we could have been twins. But I know that doesn't help you. Incidentally, have you told Peter anything of this?'

'Not yet. I will tell him—we have no secrets from each other. But I want to tell him face to face, and I want to have something concrete to tell him. David, there's an hour and a half before we get there, and I don't think I can stand the waiting!'

'I have an idea,' he said.

They had just passed a sign telling them that there

were motorway services ahead, so he slid expertly into the inside lane and drove into it. 'Do you want a drink?' she asked, puzzled. 'Petrol?'

But he drove to the farthest corner of the car park, pulled in under some overhanging trees, turned to her, put his arm round her and kissed her. That was the last thing she'd expected. His lips were pressed to hers, his hand stroking the back of her neck. What did he think he was doing? She didn't want this! But even as she tried to push him away, she realised that perhaps she did want it. It was a very comforting kiss. So she stopped pushing him, and kissed him back.

When finally he lifted his head from hers, she looked at him reproachfully. 'You only did that to make me think of something else,' she said.

'Certainly not,' he said indignantly. 'I've been thinking of nothing but that all week.'

'Well, it'll have to stop till we've made this visit.'

'As long as we can start again as soon as the visit is over.'

They looked at each other assessingly. 'Off you go,' she said. 'We're not there yet.' He sighed, and restarted the car.

After that she felt easier, and they chatted about work, about friends, about the concert being organised by Dan Webster. They enjoyed the great sweep of the moors, even the chill on top. Then they crossed the A1 and she knew it wouldn't be long. Panic returned.

Their first idea had been that David would drop her off at the garden gate, and come back for her after two hours. She changed her mind. 'David, I want you to come with me. At least to the front door. I can't do this on my own.'

'I think you probably could,' he said gently, 'but I'm

happy to come with you if you wish. How will you introduce me?'

Even then she could catch his little joke. 'I'll introduce you as a friend,' she said. 'As a friend and colleague.'

'I suppose that's better than nothing,' he said cheerfully. 'After all, things can grow.'

They turned off the motorway and drove through pretty wooded country until they came to a small town. He had memorised the road map, and drove expertly to the house. It was a pleasant street, tree-shaded, with slightly older houses and mature gardens. She looked at her watch. It was five to one.

They stopped outside a detached house, showing evidence of a keen gardener at the front. David walked round and opened her door, but she sat frozen to her seat. All she could do was look.

'Come on,' David said. 'Get out of the car and walk up the drive with a smile on your face. You can do it.' He offered her his hand to help her out.

Somehow she stumbled out of the car. Her heart was thumping but she managed a smile. He opened the gate for her, and she walked past a grey Mondeo. Ahead of her she saw the door already opening. Someone had been looking out for her. She would be speechless, there was nothing she could say. She wanted to slow down, but felt David's hand in the small of her back.

The door was open. There was a woman, a slim, smart woman with greying hair. Jane saw the face first, and the anxious expression. But she knew the face, though she hadn't seen it in twenty-nine years. And when Marion Stott saw her she smiled. 'You're my daughter,' she said, and opened her arms.

It was nine that evening before they set off back. The two hours had somehow stretched to eight. Jane sat there in the warmth of the car, listening to the throb of the engine, watching oncoming lights flash past.

'So how do you feel?' David asked as they turned onto the motorway and the car accelerated. 'I could see you were pleased you went.'

'That's one way of putting it,' she agreed.

Most of the past few hours had been spent talking and she felt the need now of a few minutes' silence. She needed to get her jumbled thoughts together. 'I'm glad I went, yes, I'm very glad I went. I like them both, and I'm pretty sure I'll like my brother and sister when I see them. But it's going to be hard for them. Meeting an older sister after being just a pair. And Mark looks just like me.'

'They seem sound, they'll cope. And your…mother will prepare them.'

Only Mrs Stott had been there when they'd arrived. There had been a tearful greeting in the hallway, and David had slid past them and had made all three of them a cup of tea. The tea things had been set out ready, and sandwiches on plates—everything prepared for Jane's arrival. Then he'd said he'd walk in the garden, take the paper and read for a while. They were to call if they needed him.

Then the two women had started to get to know each other.

'Where's the rest of the family?' Jane asked.

'Well, I thought it best if just we two met at first. I didn't want you to be overwhelmed. So Mark and Maria have gone to stay with friends. They didn't want to go but…I wanted everything to be easy for you. They've known about you since Mark turned eighteen. I thought they were entitled to know. They've been on at us to get in touch with you.'

'And where's Mr Stott?' Jane had had enough of this. 'What do Mark and Maria call you?'

Her mother looked at her unbelievingly. 'They call us Mum and Dad. Would you...? You don't mind...?'

'I don't mind. That's what you are, isn't it? The fact that I had another mum that I loved dearly doesn't matter. Now, where's Dad?'

For a while her mother's tears had stopped, but now they started again. 'He's in hospital. He desperately wanted to be here, but he couldn't be. A few months ago he started having these dreadful headaches, and then he found he was losing his balance, falling when there was no reason. At first he didn't bother, but then he went to our GP, who sent him to hospital for tests. He had a CAT scan. He's got a tumour on the brain. The consultant says it might be benign—all we can do is hope. They're going to operate on him next week.'

'I see,' said Jane. 'Look, Mum, I've scrubbed for a lot of successful brain operations. Don't give up hope. It's serious all right, but it's not necessarily bad news. Now, can we go and see him?'

There was a lot of family history to go through, so much that Jane—and her mother—wanted to know. Now, travelling home again, Jane was exhausted, but underneath she had a feeling of contentment. She had done the right thing.

Next weekend she would return, without David, to stay the night. Her brother and sister would be there to meet her. And there would be more talking, more explaining to be done.

'She was so afraid that I wouldn't want to know her,' Jane told David as the car sped through the night.

'When I heard what she went through, pregnant after just one time, no real idea of what to do, in love with my father but not able to get in touch with him, I cried myself. There was an awful lot of pressure on her to have an abortion. It could have been arranged even then. She turned it down. The aunt who brought her up was old, and just couldn't cope with the situation. She must have been so lonely, and so afraid.'

David said nothing, but stretched out a hand and stroked her arm.

'She kept asking me if I forgave her. I said of course I did. I don't know what I would have done in that situation.'

'You're a very forgiving person,' David said. 'I know that myself.'

'David Kershaw! You said that without even smiling!'

'It was meant most sincerely. But I must admit that I have a personal interest in your capacity for forgiveness.'

She waited a moment, then sighed. 'All right, I forgive you. Consider yourself forgiven.'

He unbuckled his seat belt and leaned over to kiss her on the cheek. 'You're good to me, Jane.'

'Belt up,' she snapped. 'That's what you're always shouting at me.'

'True.' He refastened his seat belt. 'So, now we carry on going out with each other?'

'If that's what you want. But just like we decided. In a casual way.'

In the darkness of the car she sensed that he turned to look at her. But he said nothing. He was still being cautious with her. She was pleased about that.

She asked him to drop her off at home, and did he

mind if she didn't invite him in? He understood. She said hello to Sue and Megan and went straight to bed. She was tired. It had been an emotionally exhausting day. But she was happy. It was good to find a new family. And it was also good to be with David again. Perhaps she'd been a bit hard on him. Just as she was going to sleep she remembered one other thing. He'd said that he loved her. *That* she would have to think about. But not now. Now she was going to sleep.

She slept soundly, and woke early and happy. All was well with the world. She would have phoned David, but he'd told her that he would be busy at the hospital all day, supervising the installation of new anaesthetic equipment, so she would have an idle, comfortable day. There had been enough emotion in her life recently to last for quite a while.

The day was fine so she decided to walk down to the corner newsagent to buy the Sunday newspapers for everyone.

'See your hospital is in trouble again,' said the newsagent, as she paid for the usual three papers. 'And there's a picture of your friend in one of them.'

She frowned at him. 'How are we in trouble?' He flicked over the pages of a copy in front of her and pointed.

Jane never bought this particular paper—ever. But a lot of people did. It made its name by buying big name exposures, or sending a team of grubby 'investigative reporters' to pry into people's lives. Then it published its findings 'in the public interest'. Jane despised the paper.

But there in front of her was the headline, CONSULTANT GETS TWO SALARIES—BUT ONLY DOES

ONE JOB. Underneath was a picture of Megan captioned, 'Junior doctor tells all.' Horrified, Jane grabbed the paper, paid and ran home.

Both Megan and Sue were asleep upstairs. Jane paused, then made two mugs of tea and went up to talk to Sue. Her friend was starting on nights later, and would normally have been left to sleep as long as she could, but this was an emergency.

'Wassermarra?' Sue mumbled. 'House on fire or something?'

'Something just as bad. Drink this tea and then look at this article.' Jane sat down on the bed as Sue reached for the tea.

The story was about Charles Grant-Liffley, one of the consultants at Emmy's. Megan worked with him, and the two girls knew that she thought she was learning from him. But there had been rumours throughout the hospital. Consultants were allowed to undertake private work as well as their National Health work, but the two had to be kept carefully apart. Perhaps Charles Grant-Liffley hadn't been careful enough. Certainly he'd left and been replaced with considerable speed.

The story was clever. There were hints, suggestions, very few real facts. But the result was to suggest that Emmy's was more interested in getting money for a few unscrupulous senior doctors than it was in treating people. 'Who knows how many women have not had the treatment they need and deserve?' the paper asked.

'What do we do?' Jane asked. 'I haven't told Megan yet.'

'Show her this, tell her to get up, pack a bag and go to the hospital. She can stay in one of the residency rooms for a while. We're going to be under seige here very shortly.'

'Under siege? What are you talking about?' Sue seemed very sure of her facts. 'I've met these reporters before. If one of them gets something the others don't have, the others rush round to see what they can pick up. There might even be a local TV crew. We can't let Megan suffer that—she's not as tough as us.'

'She's not as tough as me,' Jane said. 'You put ear-plugs in and go back to sleep. I'll get Megan off and deal with anyone who calls.'

Megan was understandably horrified by the article. 'I know who's done it,' she sobbed. 'Look, there's his byline. It's Jeremy Parks. I thought he was a friend of mine. And this picture, it's mine! He must have taken it out of my handbag.'

Suddenly, what Sue had prophesied seemed all too real. 'Get up and get dressed,' Jane said. 'Then you've got five minutes to pack a bag and drive out of here. Stay at the hospital for the next couple of nights. We'll bring you in anything you need.'

'But I've got to phone my consultant!'

'Phone him when you're in your car. Now move!'

They were only just in time. Megan had just left for the hospital when looking through the curtains, Jane saw a car draw up and park so as to carefully block their drive. A fat, unpleasant-looking man got out, walked confidently down their drive. He rang the door-bell and knocked at the same time. Jane went to open the front door.

'Good morning, I'm Roy Fuller. I'd like to speak to—'

'Move your car,' Jane interrupted. 'It's blocking our drive.'

'Well, I don't think we'll be too long, if I could just—'

'I *said* move your car.' Jane made to close the door, and the man put his hand up and held it open.

'Put your hand down or I'll phone the police, saying you're molesting me and trying to force an entry.' Jane smiled at him. 'And, please, don't think I don't mean it. Now move that car!'

The man tried to be conciliatory. 'Of course I'll move it if you want,' he said. 'Then d'you think we can talk? Are you Megan Taylor?'

'She's not here and won't be for the forseeable future,' Jane said. 'And I have nothing to say to you.' She closed the door.

She heard the man walk down the drive, and then watched him as he moved his car. He came back and rang the bell again.

'Perhaps we got off on the wrong foot,' he said. 'All I want is—'

'Look, I've told you once, no one here's going to talk to you,' Jane said. 'And you can tell that to any of your repulsive friends who come round. Now, if you ring this bell one more time, I *will* phone the police.' The man put his hand out towards the door. Jane slammed it and he just managed to move his hand in time. From behind the curtains she saw him get back into his car. But he didn't drive away.

She spent the rest of the day fending off other callers. Some were polite, and left telephone numbers or offered money. Others were less polite. But Jane knew she could cope. And it was better that she should do it than Megan. She was tougher than Megan.

She had unplugged the telephone, but at midday a call came through for her on her mobile. It was the hospital's Chief Executive Officer. 'I *am* honoured,' she said cheerfully.

'How are you coping, Miss Cabot? Have there been nuisance calls?'

'Nothing I can't deal with. A lot of reporters and people offering me money.'

'I see. Would it help if I sent down someone from Security?'

'That's the last thing we want. It'll only suggest you have something to hide. No, we can manage here. How's Megan...Dr Taylor?'

'Naturally, she's upset, but we think we can sort things out. We've called a press conference for later in the day. That should take some of the pressure off you. And thank you for what you're doing.'

'No problem,' said Jane.

Shortly afterwards, the reporters disappeared and didn't come back. Sue came down in her dressing-gown and the two sat at the kitchen table. 'I hope Megan is all right,' Sue said.

'She'll manage. I thought I had problems—but hers are bigger.' Jane's mobile rang again.

This time it was David's voice, and the very sound of it made her smile. But he was anxious. 'I've just heard what's happening,' he said. 'I'm coming round at once.'

That was the last thing she wanted. 'No, David. They've gone now, but they might be back, and if you're here it'll only cause trouble. You'll be a new face, someone else to chase. Better you stay away.' She sensed he wasn't convinced, and added, 'It'll be easier for me if you do.'

For a moment he was silent, and then he said reluctantly, 'Well, all right. But ring me on my mobile if you need me. I'm only half an hour away.'

'That's nice to hear. It really is.'

There was a further silence and Jane wondered if they'd been cut off. But then he said, 'Love you, Jane.' And then they were cut off. She was holding her own mobile but it wasn't connected so no one could hear her.

'Love you, David,' she said into the unheeding piece of plastic.

Monday morning felt good. There was no one outside the house, and Jane drove in without incident. For a while, after the two sets of exciting events over the weekend, it was difficult to remember that hospital life had to go on. But they had a full list. And she was working with David.

They were working, but they didn't have much time together. There was the special smile, the apparently accidental touch on the arm when they passed. And when they were alone in the anteroom together he stole a quick kiss.

They managed lunch together in the canteen and she told him something about the day before. He was angry. She could tell even though there was no outward sign. 'I just didn't want you round,' she insisted. 'Yes, it would have been lovely to see you, but you could only have made things worse—for all of us, as well as the hospital. You would have lost your temper. And don't try to tell me that you don't have a temper. You just shout quietly.'

'Don't you try to tell me that you're all calm, sweet and reasonable. I suspect one or two of those reporters don't know the fate they just missed.'

'Thank you,' she said demurely. 'I think that's one of the nicest things you've ever said to me.'

There was no trouble that evening, and she went to

choir practice. But the next day was different. When she met David she could tell that something had happened. He was elated, beaming at everyone.

'Why so happy?' she asked him. 'Of course, it's nice to see you happy, but is there a reason?'

'There's a reason indeed, but I want to tell you in private. Can we have a drink after work? Anywhere, any place. Just so I can ask you something.'

She looked at him suspiciously. 'If you need half an hour to ask me, then you think I'm going to need persuading. But I'm intrigued, I have to admit. Will you give me a hint?'

'No. I'll just say it's something nice. Well, I think it is. And I think that you'll think that it is. But I do need half an hour to talk to you about it.' When she still looked disbelieving he went on, 'Well, it's about going away. And that *is* all I'm going to say.'

'I'm going to my parents' next weekend, you know that.'

He gave an exasperated sigh. 'Since you don't know what I'm going to ask, you can't really refuse, can you? Can we meet in the Waggoners' Arms at about half past five tonight?'

'Waggoners' Arms it is.' She'd been there with other friends, and had found it a pleasant, suburban pub. 'But I'm busy later on.'

'Aren't you always? Incidentally, how come you can miss two hockey games in a row?'

'The university has got a star player from America who plays in my position. She's played in their Olympic team and is over here for a few weeks. I'm good, but she's tremendous. So I'm stepping down for a while.'

'Interesting,' he said thoughtfully. 'Well, I'll see you later.'

*　　*　　*

'Can you ski?' he asked her as they sat in the snug in the Waggoners'.

'Well, I went on a Scottish youth hostel trip once,' she said. 'I loved it. But I can't say I'm an expert. Are you?'

'Not expert. But I love it, too. I've done a few black slopes. Now...' He looked at her assessingly. 'You told me you've paid for Peter for the last few years. I know what nurses get, so you've never had a really good holiday, have you?'

'I haven't had a holiday away at all this year,' she said. 'I went on a counselling course with the Samaritans. But you don't need to spend money to have a good time. I've always enjoyed my holidays. Why d'you ask?'

He spread a newspaper open before her. She saw the headline, TEN FANTASTIC HOLIDAYS TO BE WON. 'Blame my mother,' he said. 'Twenty years ago she entered a competition like this and won a car. Since then she's made us all enter competitions, but no one has ever won anything big until now. I've won a skiing holiday for two.'

'I suppose you're one of those lucky people,' Jane said enviously. 'You win raffles and things like that.'

David looked sheepish. 'As a scientist, I have to say the idea of luck is foolish. On the other hand, I have to admit I've done rather well here and there. Jane, would you like to come on a skiing holiday with me?'

'A skiing holiday? With you?' She was dumbfounded. For some reason she hadn't realised that he was going to ask her.

'Why not? We fly from Manchester, take a coach up to a high village. It's earlier than most holidays, in a new, much higher resort. We stay in a five-star hotel, tuition provided and a lift pass. We could have a great time.'

'As a couple?' she asked.

'I've got no other friend I could go with. And there's no one I would rather go with than you. And…no conditions, Jane. If you want single beds, that's what we shall have. The only trouble is, it's quite soon. The weekend after next, in fact. We'd have to get our leave applications in quite fast to the hospital.'

'I need time,' she said. 'This is all a bit sudden. May I tell you tomorrow morning?'

'Tomorrow morning will be fine.'

That night she lay in bed, trying to make up her mind. Her first reaction was that she wouldn't go. Certainly she would really like a skiing holiday, and she'd like to be with David. But that would mean that she had to… She knew that he'd meant what he'd said, that they could have single beds if she wanted. And so far she had nearly slept with him…was it three times?

She liked David. No. She sighed. She loved him. Had she joined a long line of women who had done the same, only to be told that they'd agreed that the relationship was only ever going to be a temporary one?

He meant so much to her. He meant more than John Gilmore ever had. And he said he loved her, claimed to have said that to only one other woman in his life. Well, perhaps. She was still wary.

She was twenty-nine. Up till this moment she hadn't realised it, but she was dissatisfied with her life. She liked her job, enjoyed singing in the choir, working for the Samaritans, playing hockey. She was acquiring a new family. But all that wasn't enough. She wanted David. But she was afraid that he might leave her.

She would go skiing with him. What had she to lose? Her heart was lost already.

CHAPTER EIGHT

JANE booked the necessary ten days off next morning, and then told the surgeon, 'I hope you manage to get a good substitute, Edmund.'

'Hmm,' he grunted. 'I suppose I'll have to. But it's going to be rough. Young David's just told me he's going skiing at the same time. Where are you going?'

She didn't like lying, so she temporised. 'I've just come across some relations in Yorkshire. I'm going to spend some time with them.' Well, it was true.

Just then David entered the anteroom, already gowned. 'Everyone's deserting me,' Edmund said. 'Our scrub nurse here is going away at the same time as you. I should have booked a holiday myself.'

She saw David looking at her, his expression neutral. She gave him a tiny nod. 'I'm sure you'll cope,' David said to Edmund. 'And it's good to let others have a chance to work with you. We all need a change from time to time. I'm ready for the op when you are.'

Jane didn't have a chance to speak to David in private until that afternoon, when she was helping him with the pre-op inspections. 'I'm so glad you're coming,' he said in a low voice. 'I take it you are coming with me?'

'If you still want me. But it's got to remain an absolute secret. No one but we two is to know about it. You can give me a list of what I'll need to take and I'll meet you at the airport. I'll take my car there.'

'I was going to go by taxi,' he said. 'Are you sure you don't want to share it? It would be easier on you.'

'I'm certain, thank you. We'll meet there.'

He looked up from the notes he was making. 'You seem defensive,' he said. 'Are you sure I've not talked you into something you're not certain about? I really wouldn't want that, you know. And as I said, you can guess what I want, but the options are entirely up to you. I do mean that.'

She looked at him. She still wasn't sure whether he was a genuinely nice person or just trying to salve his own conscience. 'Remember Ann Deeds?' she asked. 'She always said you were fair with her.'

He shrugged. 'I'm trying to be honest, Jane. And you mean an awful lot more to me than she did.'

For a while they stared at each other in silence, then she told him, 'You mean a lot to me, too, but I'm still not sure that it's a good idea.'

They were standing in the sister's room, just the two of them. He moved past her and opened the door. 'No one in the corridor!' he said. 'We're alone!' Then he grabbed her and kissed her.

After a while he leaned back, though he was still holding her round the waist. 'We're going on our holidays together,' he said, 'and I *am* looking forward to it. If you break your leg—too bad!'

'If I break my leg while I'm supposed to be in Yorkshire,' she told him, 'I'll break your neck.' She leaned forward to kiss him. 'But I'm looking forward to it as well.'

There was a line to be drawn. She wouldn't lie to Megan or Sue. There had been no more trouble from reporters, and Megan had moved back home, so one evening when they were all together she told them.

'We're not going to try to talk you out of it,' Megan

said calmly. 'You're a big girl now, and you can make your own decisions. Mind you, I thought I was able to make my own decisions. I trusted a man and look where it got me. Dead trouble at work. But I agree, yours is a different case.'

'Have you been pressurised at all?' Sue asked, also calmly. 'And remember, there are more kinds of pressure than just saying that you love each other so why not? Has he tried to make you feel guilty?'

'No, there's been no pressure. He's been really good that way.'

'Fine. What are you doing about contraception? Contraception is part of my work as a midwife. I'd better have a word with you about it. He may be as careful as you want him to be, but in things like this it's always better not to have to rely on other people.'

Surprisingly, this extremely sensible suggestion was the thing that came closest to making her change her mind, though it wasn't intended to. But she didn't change her mind. And she did take Sue up on her offer.

Surprisingly, when she went to Yorkshire that weekend, she found herself also confiding what she was doing to her new mum. Marion was very thoughtful.

'Are you sure he only wants a casual relationship, Jane?' she asked. 'I know I had a lot to think about last weekend, but I would have said that he…cared for you a lot. He looked at you when you weren't looking at him. And it was definitely a loving look.'

Her new father was doing well. His tumour had been found to be benign. She managed to hit it off straight away with her new brother and sister, though they were—perhaps inevitably—a bit cautious.

When she drove back across the Pennines late on Sunday, she was conscious of her life changing. She now had a family other than Peter. There was David—and where would that relationship lead? She realised she had been in a happy rut, but now things were bound to change. For the better, she hoped.

Jane loved airports. She had flown from Manchester before, on a late season package holiday, and the romance of flying had not yet left her. She liked the bustle, the feeling of excitement.

As arranged, she met David in the great hall by the ticket office. He was dressed for the outdoors in anorak, woollen sweater, thick trousers and boots. She was dressed similarly in her walking gear.

They exchanged a quick kiss. 'You look the part,' he said. 'But have you packed for après-ski? There's quite a night life, you know.'

'Try telling any woman not to pack for après-ski.' She indicated the two heavy bags she had just pushed in on a trolley. 'Those aren't full of boots and sweaters, you know. I've bought all sorts of gorgeous new stuff.'

'Then here's a bit more. Is there room in a bag for this?' He gave her a packet of shiny expensive-looking blue paper.

'What's in here?' She was curious.

'It's a present, but you can open it now if you want.'

She loved surprise presents, and hastily ran her thumb down the seam of the packet. Inside was something in a scarlet material, very soft to the touch. She shook it out. It was an all-in-one ski suit, and she thought it very fetching.

'The latest thing in ski outfits,' he told her. 'You'll look wonderful in it.'

'You shouldn't buy me clothes! I can buy my own.'

'I told you, I won the holiday. I can afford to buy

you something extra. Now, stuff it in a case, and let's get the bags checked in.'

Even the queuing wasn't too bad. Then she enjoyed the wait, the masses of magazines and books, the coffee apparently every twenty minutes. Finally they boarded the plane.

Once they were in the air she took his hand. 'Thank you for bringing me,' she said. 'You've no idea how much I'm looking forward to it. And being with you.'

She appreciated her anorak when they landed. The temperature was so much colder than home. They were efficiently shepherded through customs and onto a lux-urious coach, which set off on the long, winding journey up into the mountains. Their first sight of the white-peaked Alps was breathtaking.

The road grew steeper, the snow piled up on each side deeper. Their driver pulled up in a little village, and had a shouted conversation with the driver of the largest snow-plough she had ever seen. It was too fast for her schoolgirl French, but David seemed able to fol-low.

'The driver's worried about keeping the road clear,' he said. 'Apparently there's been more snow than usual—and he thinks there may be avalanches.'

'Surely they should be used to that sort of thing by now?'

David shrugged. 'We're going to a new ski village, quite a bit higher than most. It's at the end of a new road. The driver's just a bit apprehensive.'

A man in a seat ahead of them turned and winked. In an expansive American accent he said, 'Don't get alarmed. Around here, worrying about snow conditions is what they do. It's like Englishmen talking about the weather.'

'I'm relieved to hear it,' said Jane.

The coach drove on, over the most slender of bridges. The driver explained on his PA system that the bridge had just been built, and was considered a triumph of engineering. It was the only way to the new village that was their destination. Jane peered out of the window and winced at the drop to the stream far below.

When they'd left the airport the weather had been sunny, but now the skies grew dark grey, and flurries of snow flattened against the windows. Soon they were in a snowstorm, and the coach's windscreen wipers were working at double speed. 'What do we do if it's snowing like this when we want to go skiing?' she asked David.

'You've heard of après-ski? That's in the evening. Well, there's also devant-ski. That's during the day. You just drink and they close the shutters to persuade you that it's night-time. Alternatively, we could just stay in bed. Ow!'

'That's the elbow I use to fend off people who tackle me a little roughly.' She smiled sweetly. 'Remember, I'm an outdoor girl. I take my sport seriously. If I can't ski, then I want to do something else.'

'No problem. There's a gym, a swimming pool, a sauna and a skating rink. For you they'll probably find a boxing ring.'

She took his hand and squeezed it. 'After all that I'll really enjoy my après-ski.'

They both looked out of the window. All that could be seen were the swirling flakes of snow.

She had never experienced such luxury as there was at the hotel. The bus stopped under a great wooden canopy. There was a moment of bone-chilling cold as they dashed across to the door, and then all was warm again. There were polished wooden floors and walls, decorative plants, the distant tinkling of a piano and the soft rumble of conversation. This was civilisation, far removed from the starkness of the elements outside.

They checked in and went up to their room. That, too, was luxurious, furnished tastefully with flowers, a television and a mini-bar. Their bags were brought up. 'We're on holiday, Jane,' he said.

She looked out of the heavily glazed window. Outside she could see the blurred outline of mountain peaks—she thought. The relentless snowfall hid it all. What about the vision she'd had of skiing down snowy but sun-drenched slopes? People came back with a sun-tan after skiing. Not in this. But that was for tomorrow.

For the first time she felt a touch of unease. In the past, on the few occasions when David and she had...when she had nearly...when they had almost...well, there had been a sort of leading up to it. She could think about it happily now. She loved David, and guessed he loved her. But they weren't lovers yet. And she felt a little uneasy.

In his uncanny way, he guessed what she was thinking. He came up behind her, took her shoulders in his hands and kissed her lightly on the back of the neck. 'It doesn't matter, sweetheart,' he said. 'You're tired, you don't have to make any decisions at all. Look, we even have twin beds.'

That decided her. 'We can always push them together,' she said sturdily.

There were a couple of hours before dinner was served. They decided to go for a walk to explore the village. 'It won't take much exploring,' he told her. 'There are four hotels, the foundations of a couple more and a handful of houses. The ski lifts, of course, and a road in and a road out. Up to a couple years ago there was only an old farm or two. This is all new construction.'

'So where does the road out go to?'

'Surprisingly, there's a little village a few kilometres up the valley. That isn't a holiday place, it's an old high farming village. It's called Vallere. And after that…just mountains.'

'Let's go see what we can.'

He'd advised her what to bring, what to buy, and she wrapped up as he told her. They carried their boots down to the lobby and put them on, sitting on the benches provided. Then they ventured outside.

It was like walking into a deep freeze with a gale blowing through it. The snowflakes were hard little chips of ice, and they bit into the exposed skin of her face. When she breathed in, the cold was dragged into her lungs, chilling her from inside. She put her head down, forced her shoulders into the wind and they walked to the end of the village. It wasn't far. Then they walked back. They had seen no other walkers. No one else was foolish enough to venture out. David put his arm round her shoulders, stooping to peer into the hood of her anorak. 'Had enough?' he bellowed.

'Exercise for today over,' Jane shouted back. 'Let's go and get changed.'

She delighted in the free toiletries that the hotel put out in its bathrooms, this hotel's range being larger than most. A hair-drier was also provided, and that, too, was a blessing although she had brought a portable one from home.

Jane had the first bath, then sat in front of the dressing-table, blowing and brushing her hair while David bathed. There was still a residual shyness between them, so she had undressed in the bathroom, and when she came out he was in his dressing-gown.

She knew that après-ski in this hotel was smart. She went to some trouble with her hair, and then put on a sleeveless blue silk top and a long black skirt. David came out of the bathroom in a white shirt and light-weight grey trousers. 'Jane, you look stunning!'

'You can kiss me a little bit,' she said. 'I haven't put on my make-up yet.'

So he did. And he wasn't going to stop.

'I said kiss me a little bit!' She looked at her watch. 'Come on, get your jacket on. We're going to be late for dinner and I'm famished.'

He shook his head in disbelief. 'I bring a woman away on a romantic holiday. I kiss her, and what does she say? ''We're going to be late for dinner.'''

'A girl needs her strength,' she told him demurely, and then blushed.

He put on a floral tie and then his jacket, and they went down to dinner. His suit was the lightest of well-cut grey flannels, and she thought he looked fantastic in it. Other people thought so, too, and she was aware of admiring glances from the women—and some of the men—as they accepted a glass of champagne in the bar.

At times she was entranced by his good looks, especially since he seemed to think so little of them himself. At other times he was just her David, the man she loved and who loved her, and she was mildly surprised to see other people attracted to him, too.

Their meal was French, not English. Perhaps some of the ingredients were the same, but the effect was entirely different. There seemed to be a multitude of tiny courses, each one delightful but not entirely filling. 'It's a big warm plate for such a tiny pie,' she said as a pastry was put in front of her. It looked rather lonely but it smelled delicious. There were wisps of salad round it, but that was all.

'Just try it,' he said. 'Eat it slowly.'

She did. The pastry was filled with seafood in the most delicate of white sauces. The sharpness of the rocket salad round it made it even more tasty. 'This is so good,' she mumbled.

There were wines to go with the meal. Jean-Claude, the *maître d'hôtel*, had discussed the choice with David. In fact, they'd had a long chat. Then she had been somewhat appalled to find he'd ordered three bottles. 'We'll never get through those,' she gasped.

'Don't worry. They'll be recorked and we can drink them tomorrow night. You don't have to finish a bottle, you know.'

'You do in the parties I've been to,' she said glumly. But this was different.

They finished the meal with tiny coffees. Jane was aware that she had enjoyed every mouthful but was not in the least over-full. It had been a wonderful meal. Part of the enjoyment had been because of the efforts of Jean-Claude, who had been all that a *maître d'hôtel* should have been. Just before their coffees were served, they saw a worried-looking waiter whisper to Jean-Claude, and then he was gone. 'The cook's dropped salt in the ice cream,' she suggested.

They had a last drink at the bar, chatted to some of the other guests and speculated about the weather the next day. Jane noticed that there were more than a few women who apparently wanted David's opinion. He's

mine, she thought smugly. And we're going to bed together soon.

They were going to part the next day. David was a
reasonably expert skiier, and he was going to the top,
but it had been arranged that Jane should have a couple
of lessons on the nursery slopes.

'I'll think I'll stay with you,' he'd said.

'You'll do no such thing! You'll get on the slopes
you're fit for. David, this isn't negotiable—you're skiing while I'm learning!'

'But I want to be with you!'

'We'll be together at night.'

So they agreed. And she was happy with it.

He held her hand as they walked up to their bedroom.
Once inside he took off his jacket and loosened his tie.
Unselfconsciously, she pulled her top over her head and
unfastened her skirt. She stepped out of it. She hadn't
bothered with tights. Clad solely in new black briefs
and bra, she walked over to the window, lifted the blind
and peered out. There was a rustle of clothes behind
her. Perhaps David was putting on the grey silk dressing-gown he had thrown on the bed.

'Jane, I think every man in this hotel is envying me
now.'

'If they are, every woman is envying me. David, we
won't ski in this, will we?'

He joined her at the window, standing behind her,
and looked out. 'No. we won't ski in this. We'll wait
and hope the weather clears.'

She let the blind drop into place but didn't turn round.
She was aware of his body behind hers, close but not
touching. His longing for her was so strong that she
thought she could feel it. Her own skin pricked with
delight and anticipation.

When he first did touch her she sighed. It was the most gentle of touches, his fingertips straying down the long strands of her hair. He caressed her shoulders, gently kneading the muscles, and his thumbs ran down the long valley of her back.

She didn't want to turn round, didn't want to do anything. She wanted to be done to. Later, perhaps, she would be a willing and inventive lover, but for now he could do to her what he wished. She knew she was giving him pleasure. There was the warmth of his breath on her back and she could tell by its rapidity how she was exciting him.

Deftly, he unclipped her bra, then slid the lace garment from her shoulders so that it fell to the floor. Then his hands reached downwards, round her, and gently cupped the heaviness of her breasts. Her breasts *were* heavy. As his hands held her she felt her skin tauten, the pink tips harden.

He pulled her back towards him, and she gasped as she realised that he was naked. The fine hair on his chest rasped excitingly on her back, and she was suddenly made more aware of his great need for her. Now she would move. She clutched his hands harder to her and leaned backwards so that all of her body was pressed against his.

He turned her. Swiftly, almost brutally, his head swooped to hers and she opened her mouth to the force of his kiss. She could feel his urgency, and her own body responded to it. She clutched at his back, pulling herself against him, trying to get even closer to him. She wanted to—

He lifted his head, and she looked up to see the passion in his face slipping away, to be replaced by anger. Now she, too, heard what he had—a frenzied knocking on their bedroom door. One thing was certain. Someone wasn't going to go away.

He bent his head to kiss her quickly again. 'Wait in the bathroom,' he whispered, and almost unthinkingly she moved towards the door. She saw him stride to the bed to shrug on his dressing-gown.

She hadn't yet unpacked her own dressing-gown, but there were complimentary robes in the bathroom so she pulled on one of those. Then she decided she wasn't going to cower there. Whatever it was that was so urgent, she wanted to know about it herself. She walked back into the bedroom.

David was talking to Jean-Claude. No longer was he dressed in the impeccable black and white of his trade. Instead, he was wearing breeches and the thickest of sweaters. His attire altered his image completely. Now he looked a tough man of the outdoors. And he was worried.

'Pardon, mam'selle, m'sieur, this is an unwarrantable intrusion,' he said quickly. 'But you are, I believe, a doctor, a nurse?'

Jane saw the anger slip from David's face, to be replaced by concern. Now she was worried as well. Only the most dire of emergencies would have caused them to be disturbed in a hotel such as this.

'I am a doctor, Miss Cabot is a nurse, yes. Is there a problem?'

'There is a great problem.' Jean-Claude had been schooled not to show emotion, so it was all the more shocking to see the fear and anger on his face.

'The weather, the snowfall, it is most, most unusual. And so…we have had avalanches. I do not know what will become of this hotel, but the road below us is cut off. The new bridge—it has been swept away. And further up the valley, the village of Vallere, it has been almost destroyed. There has been no avalanche like this for hundreds of years. Many homes destroyed, people killed or lost, many are injured. And we cannot get help in by road because of the destroyed bridge. And we cannot fly help in because of the visibility.'

'You need medical help?' David asked.

'We need it urgently. We need all kinds of help. You will come?'

'Arrange transport. We'll be downstairs in fifteen minutes.'

CHAPTER NINE

'ONE minute,' David said. He knelt in front of Jane, opened her robe and wrapped his arms round her waist. Then he kissed each of her breasts. The emotions, the feelings of ten minutes before flashed back instantly, but both knew there was nothing they could do, just enjoy the one minute he had allowed them. It was soon past.

'Come on,' she said, pulling him to his feet, 'we've got work to do. Shall I pack something?'

'Bring your bad-weather gear. And anything that you won't mind getting blood or dirt on. There'll be no uniform up there.'

'Great,' she said sadly, surveying the wardrobe full of her newest and most treasured clothes.

'Better bring a toothbrush, too. I don't think we're going to be back here all that quickly.'

The enormity of what had happened was just getting through to her. 'What about medical supplies? We've got nothing. Well, I've got a bag with aspirins and plaster and so on, but that's all.'

'There should be some kind of medical station up there. We'll just have to hope.'

They were quickly dressed, and packed a bag each. Downstairs the lobby looked completely different. Instead of the well-dressed guests at the bar there were worried locals in their climbing gear. Jean-Claude came over to meet them. 'We must set off at once. It is possible that the road between here and Vallere will soon

158

be blocked, there are no snow ploughs here. We must get there in time.'

He shepherded them out and they climbed up into some kind of four-wheel-drive vehicle. Its engine was already running. Jean-Claude slid behind the wheel, and with a noisy clashing of gears they set off. 'Bit different from the vehicle we arrived in,' David murmured.

Jane stared over Jean-Claude's shoulder. The headlights were of little use—all that could be seen was the swirling of snowflakes. The ride was rough. Sometimes they bumped over unseen obstacles, at other times the vehicle would skid madly. She appreciated how good a driver Jean-Claude was. If anything, they were too hot. But no one suggested turning the heat down.

'I want to know what to expect,' she said quietly. 'Have you ever worked in this kind of operation before?'

'Once, many years ago, just after I'd qualified. There was a bus crash miles from anywhere in Scotland, and I helped the local GP. This is different from ordinary medicine. You don't try to treat anyone. Basically, you start with triage, sorting out those who desperately need attention, those who will need it soon and those who can wait. Then you aim solely to stabilise, to make sure people don't get worse. And you arrange for people to go to hospital by ambulance, in the proper order.' His voice was doubtful. 'But if what Jean-Claude says is true, there'll be no chance of getting people out.'

'Who will be in charge? You?'

'I hope not. It's important that there's someone in overall control, who looks after the communications and the transport as well as the medical care. If we can't get people evacuated inside twenty-four hours, there'll be the problem of feeding people and finding them somewhere to sleep as well. This is ultimately a logistical problem—it has to be run like a military operation.'

'So I tell people what I'm good for, and then do as I'm told?'

He put his arm round her and squeezed her. 'Have you ever done as you were told?'

They were silent for a while, then she said, 'Not half an hour ago we were ready for bed. We've had a long day. But now I feel ready for action. I'm not tired at all.'

'Adrenaline,' he told her. 'I suspect you're going to be running on it for some time. Incidentally, do you know about the golden hour?'

She'd heard the expression. 'It's about what you do after an accident, isn't it?'

'It's the time between trauma taking place and the definitive treatment of it. If there's only an hour between an accident and the patient being in Theatre, he or she has a good chance. Any delay longer than an hour and the patient's chances go down. Now we're going to have to stretch that hour into hours or even days. It's going to be hard.'

They arrived at Vallere. Ahead of them they saw someone waving a torch, who directed the vehicle to the back of a large wooden building. 'Village hall,' Jean-Claude said. 'Fortunately well out of the path of the avalanche. We'll use it as our emergency centre. It was designed for this purpose.'

They scrambled out of the vehicle and rushed for the door. Inside was a sports hall, with great overarching wooden beams. Sitting at the side of the room, clustered in groups, there were people, oddly quiet except for those who moaned or cried. They were in shock. Some lay strangely still on the floor. There were two or three young people carrying round trays of warm drinks.

Jane saw a woman clutching her arm, in obvious pain. It seemed to be dislocated. She made to go over to the woman but David pulled her back. 'Do as you're asked,' he said. 'That woman will have been assessed. If we all do what we feel like, the result will be chaos.'

'I don't like passing someone in pain if I can help.'

'You're going to help people in pain. Now, didn't you once tell me you had training on a burns unit?'

'Yes. Why? I won't say I liked it, but I think I was good at it.' The work on the burns unit had been hard, often horrifying, but ultimately satisfying.

'Surprisingly, there are often a lot of burns after an avalanche. People get swept onto stoves, pushed against cookers. It's odd but it's true.'

Jean-Claude led them behind a set of screens and whispered quickly to a young, fit-looking man, looking rather lost in a white coat obviously not his. The young man looked up, delight spreading across his face. In accented English he said, 'Welcome, David and Jane. I am Maurice. I am a doctor now for nearly a year. If you will help us, we will be glad.'

Jane's heart went out to him. This obviously unsure young man could have been her brother Peter.

Another, much older man came through, calmer than Maurice and with better English. 'I am Dr Berfay,' he said. 'I am in charge here. And you are?'

Quickly David ran through his qualifications and Jane's as well, mentioning her experience as a burns nurse.

Dr Berfay allowed himself a small smile. 'I doubt we will have need of an anaesthetist, but your skills as a doctor will be most valuable. Nurse Cabot, we have eight people suffering from burns. Will you do what you can for them? Dr Leclerc will show you where our materials are stored. Then, please, report to me.'

Maurice—presumably Dr Leclerc—pulled her sleeve and led her to a little cloakroom where she could scrub up, and showed her a cupboard with everything she might need for the emergency treatment. For the smallest of burns there was cream, but she knew that for anything more serious cream was the last thing she would need. There were sterile dressings and cling film for the worst cases.

'Dr Berfay seems very organised,' she said to Maurice.

'Dr Berfay was once a soldier. He has seen action in many parts of the world. His skills here are very good.'

She remembered what David had said about the golden hour. It was time to start work. 'I can manage now, Maurice,' she said, and he led her to the screened-off area where the burns cases were lying.

She walked round and glanced quickly at every injury, being careful to keep her features calm. Then she made her choice.

There were two children, one with extensive burns to the arms, the other to the chest. They had been brought in together, apparently caught and scalded by a pot of soup on a stove. They were in considerable pain. She examined them quickly, and decided that the injuries weren't life-threatening. They were superficial partial-thickness burns. The skin was red and moist, with a granular appearance. Cream would do, and the comfort of their mother, who was sitting by them, still terrified. Jane tried to reassure her, and then went on to the next case.

This one was bad. It was a woman with a deep burn

over the abdomen. She had been pressed against a stove. Jane assessed the damaged area as just under fifteen per cent, and noted with dismay that the woman wasn't complaining of too much pain. That was a bad sign. Jane knew there would have been massive plasma loss, so she set up a giving set and arranged for an infusion of Hartmann's solution. That should expand the plasma. But Jane knew that the woman needed expert medical care, preferably in a dedicated burns unit. Here, she would just have to take her chance.

It was difficult to take a case history as she spoke very little French, but somehow she managed. The rest of her patients appeared at first not to be too seriously ill, and she was able to act as a normal nurse, treating injuries and offering care and sympathy. For pain relief there were two intravenous injections of nalbuphine.

There was one last thing she was worried about. She knew that inhalation injury was now the commonest cause of death in burns. She'd examined all of her patients for burns round the lips and singed nasal hair, and checked breathing constantly. Wheezing, excessive coughing, signs of respiratory distress—all were danger signs. But this time she appeared to be in luck.

Only on the third inspection did she come to suspect it. It was a man with superficial burns on his back, showing a long crooked red line. Jane carefully cut the shirt and sweater away from the burn, then placed clean cold-water compresses over the charred cloth. The man was lying, of course, on his chest.

When she stooped to look at his face she found his pupils dilated, and he had cyanosis of the lips. He seemed to have lapsed into a coma. Jane tried to take a history from those around her, asking just how had the man been injured. It was hard, speaking in broken

French and broken English, but eventually she picked
up the words 'car exhaust', and gathered what had happened.

A car, with its engine running, had been turned on
its side by the avalanche. A further fall had pressed the
victim against the exhaust pipe—the engine had still
been running—hence the long crooked burn. However,
it had been some time before the man had been dug
out—he'd been completely covered by snow. She
guessed then what was wrong. The man was suffering
from carbon monoxide poisoning, having inhaled the
exhaust fumes.

Quickly, she fetched the cylinder, fixed on the mask
and gave him one hundred per cent oxygen. He also
needed to be transferred to a specialist unit, but he'd
have to take his chances.

For the moment there was little more she could do
with her little group. In hospital she would never have
dreamed of leaving them, but this was still an emergency situation.

She found Maurice outside her little area and told him
she thought she could be free for half an hour so should
she report to Dr Berfay?

'Dr Berfay and your Dr David, they are setting a leg.
The bone is…how you say…? It has damaged the flesh,
there is more than one piece broken.'

'A comminuted fracture,' Jane said, wincing.

'Dr Berfay is very glad that David can give the anaesthetic and perhaps help. The patient is an old man.
With two doctors perhaps he will be lucky. But now
perhaps you will help me? There are some ladies I have
to examine, and perhaps I will need some help with
bandaging.'

They worked through the night. They had three doctors and an abundance of willing but unskilled helpers. She was the only trained nurse. After a while she found that she was supervising the helpers, rather than nursing. It wasn't ideal but it was the only thing to do.

Once or twice she saw David. They smiled at each other, but didn't stop to talk. There was work to be done.

Dawn came, just a gradual lightening of the dark. The snowstorm was as heavy as ever. Jean-Claude came to find her. Apparently, he was supervising the cooking of food and the sleeping arrangements. 'I think you should sleep now,' he said.

'I'm all right, Jean-Claude. Good for a few hours yet.'

He shook his head. 'It is not enough to be good for a few more hours. This situation may last for days. There is no way of getting our patients down the road. The bridge is down and the army is trying to erect another one. No helicopters dare try to land. We are…I think the word is marooned.'

'Just a couple of hours, then.'

'I have a meal for you by your bed. Soup, bread, cheese.' He shuddered. 'What a way to feed my guests! But it is fuel, not food.'

In fact, it was marvellous. She was to sleep in a campbed in yet another corner of the main room, partitioned off by screens. This was the doctors' quarters. There were three campbeds there. She took off the trainers she'd been wearing instead of boots, and lay on the bed fully dressed. Within seconds she was asleep.

Jane became aware that someone was leaning over her, and she woke to find it was David. He looked tired. His hair was in a mess, he needed a shave and he smelled, half of man, half of hospital. And she thought she'd never seen him look more lovable. She reached up and pulled him down to her.

'This isn't quite the holiday I'd planned,' he said.

'It's not quite the holiday I expected. But I'm with you—well, some of the time—and I'm happy. David, you look all in.'

'I'm going to get into your bed. Unfortunately, you're going to get out of it. Are you still up to this, Jane?'

'Watch it, matey! I'm a nurse. We carry on when all around us doctors falter and fail. Yes, I'm up to this.' She wriggled out of bed. 'I need five minutes in the bathroom, then I'm ready for work.' She looked sadly at the once good shirt and trousers she was wearing. 'I don't think they've got a clean uniform for me, though.'

He kissed her, and she hugged him. 'Love you, sweetheart,' he said. She went to pick up her bag. When she turned to look at him he was already asleep.

Jean-Claude found her a piece of bread and a cup of coffee. He told her that the weather was still as bad and there was still no hope of relief. She reported to Dr Berfay for duty. He asked her to go with Maurice, look first at those with burns and then help with the rest of the patients.

'This is now becoming a nursing not a medical situation,' he told her. 'A few more injured were brought in while you were asleep, but I doubt there will be more. Those not yet discovered will be dead. We must hold out as best we can until we are relieved.'

He did make it sound like a military operation, but she realised that this attitude was necessary. It prevented chaos, helped save lives.

There were only seven now in the little burns section. The man with the burn to his back, with possible carbon-monoxide poisoning, had gone. She looked at Maurice questioningly.

He shrugged and spread his hands. 'In hospital, perhaps with the right equipment, he might have lived. You—we—did all that was possible. It was not enough.'

She didn't have the energy to spare to grieve. 'The rest look reasonable,' she said. 'I'll change dressings and so on, and then come to find you.'

There had been some changes made while she'd been asleep. Those who were only mildly injured, or suffering from shock, had been moved to another building. There was no longer the background noise of screams or sobbing so it came as a bit of a shock to hear shouting, and then the sound of a scream. She looked over, and saw that someone new had been brought in.

Dr Berfay had at long last gone to sleep. Only she and Maurice were on duty. And she could tell from a distance that Maurice wasn't happy. She knew she shouldn't interfere until asked, but something about the woman's screams made her incapable of keeping away.

The patient was a woman of about twenty-five. And her distended abdomen made it obvious she was about to give birth. Maurice was bent over, listening with a Pinard's stethoscope for foetal distress, but Jane knew what was wrong. Emmy's was a women's hospital, and she had seen a vast number of pregnant women brought into Theatre. The signs were obvious.

'How long has she been in labour?' she asked Maurice.

'Twenty-four hours. This is her first child, but...'

Maurice had witnessed perhaps a couple of dozen births, while she had helped with literally hundreds. Here she was the expert. She conducted a swift internal examination and realised what was wrong at once—a deep transverse arrest. Quite simply, the baby was stuck. 'This woman needs a Caesarean section—quickly. Shall I wake up David and ask him to do it?'

Maurice would be good in time. 'Certainly,' he said. 'I do not now feel quite competent. I will have her carried to where we can operate.'

David looked so peaceful asleep. She looked at him once, then leaned over and shook him vigorously. Bewildered, he opened his eyes. He had been asleep an hour.

'David, there's a woman who needs a section right now. You'll have to do it.'

His eyes focussed and she saw him take in the message. He swung his feet off the bed. 'I'll wash my face and be with you in two minutes,' he said. 'Be a good scrub nurse and lay out what I'll need.'

Caesarean sections were often performed quickly. There wasn't the full equipment necessary for swift anaesthesia so David gave a spinal block. It was tricky, but somehow he managed it. Then Jane rushed through the necessary procedures before the operation began. She winced as she cut corners, missed precautions that, in a hospital, would have been second nature. But this wasn't a hospital. It was a battlefield.

The cut was made, David gently parted the membranes, reached in and lifted out the baby. Jane acted as midwife while Maurice acted as scrub nurse. She took the slippery, feebly yelling little mite and laid it—no, not it, laid her—on the table which had been all they'd been able to find to act as a cot. The baby looked good.

She stepped up to the mother's head, smiled down at the desperate face and said, '*C'est une petite fille. Elle est belle.'* The mother smiled, and Jane looked up to see both David and Maurice silently laughing.

The storm continued, unabated, and still no one could reach them. As Dr Berfay had said, they were now more concerned with nursing than medicine. There were many offers of help, but all had to be carefully supervised. She fell into a routine, and for the next four days she worked regular nineteen-hour days. David did the same.

She saw little of him. There was the chance of an odd kiss, a hug occasionally, but mostly they worked.

She had never been so tired. Then one morning there came the roar of engines outside and the sound of cheering. She stared uncomprehendingly as tough-looking men in uniform came through the front door.

From somewhere David came over and put his arm round her. 'The professionals have arrived,' he said. 'Now we can go home.'

The handover didn't take too long. There were quick goodbyes and thanks. She kissed Maurice, the doctor who'd had a baptism of fire in the past five days. Dr Berfay was staying, and he looked happy to be among his old compatriots. Ambulances took the more serious cases away first, and then Jean-Claude, a vastly different man from the dapper *maître d'hôtel* they'd first met, drove them back down to his hotel. It was four in the afternoon.

'It would be an honour for me,' Jean-Claude said, 'if you would come down to dinner in…when shall we say?'

'A couple of hours,' she said promptly. 'I need to have a bath first, and not just an ordinary bath but a long, long soak. And my hair!'

'In two hours' time, then.' He indicated his stained

clothes. 'I shall myself find it pleasant to dress properly.'

The clothes she had been wearing were bundled into a plastic bag. On the bed she laid out the teddy Sue had bought her and a new dress. Her make-up was ready on the dressing-table. And all this time the bath was filling.

As he passed, David bent over to kiss her. 'No!' she commanded. 'Not yet. I'm tired, dirty and smelly. You can kiss me when I've joined the human race again.'

He kissed her anyway. 'I don't care how dirty you are,' he said.

The bath was sheer bliss. She poured the luxurious hotel bath oil into it and David brought her a cup of tea to drink. For half an hour she just lay there, feeling the weariness ease out of her body. When she'd entered the bedroom she'd still been hyper and, even though fatigued, her body and mind had still been ready to work. Now the excitement left her. There was nothing more for her to do.

Eventually she sat up, reached for the hand spray and washed her hair. She mustn't be too selfish. David would need a bath as well. Wrapping one towel round her hair and one round her body, she walked back into the bedroom. Now she knew why he hadn't come to talk to her. Dressed in his gown, he was asleep on the bed.

'Bath-time, David,' she whispered. 'Wake up.'

He blinked up at her. 'Not asleep,' he mumbled. 'Just… I'll have a bath.'

They went down to dinner, as they'd intended to do every evening, a well-dressed couple in a luxury hotel. They were met by Jean-Claude, now as dapper as ever in black and white. He conducted them to their table, reverently produced a dark bottle and showed the label to David.

'We have been keeping a dozen of these for a special occasion,' he said. 'I believe this is a special occasion.'

David looked aghast. 'But, Jean-Paul, that's a vintage…'

Jean-Paul deftly drew the cork and poured two glassfuls. 'This is with my compliments. It is a small gesture to thank you for what you have done.'

'Then sit down and have a glass of it with us.'

Jean-Paul looked horrified. 'I could not sit in my own dining room!'

'Please,' Jane said. 'We'd really like you to.'

So, ill at ease, Jean-Claude sat with them.

She tasted the wine, doing what David did, smelling it then holding it in her mouth before swallowing. At first it was just wine, but then…she knew that the four-pound bottles of red from the supermarket would never be the same again.

The meal was a delight. After the adequate but ordinary food she'd had for the past few days, it was a revelation. And she enjoyed the feeling of luxury, the unobtrusive service, the candles on the table, the shine of glass and silver.

At the end of the meal Jean-Claude came over and said, 'There are messages for you, Dr Kershaw, from your hospital.'

'Lose them,' David said. 'We're going back tomorrow. I'll bother about the hospital then.'

He turned to her. 'That was a wonderful meal. Shall we round it off with an Armagnac at the bar?'

'No. But I want you to have one. I'll go to bed. See you there.'

'In ten minutes,' he said.

Jean-Claude served David the brandy, once again with the compliments of the house. David sipped the rich, warm liquid and smiled.

Earlier that day he'd thought he couldn't be more tired, and all he'd wanted had been to go to bed and sleep for a week. But, as a doctor, he'd been tired before. And the meal he'd just had, the wine and now the brandy, had reinvigorated him. And upstairs, waiting for him, was Jane. He no longer felt tired.

There were arrangements to check for the next day, but Jean-Claude assured him that all was in hand. He finished his brandy and walked upstairs.

Jane was waiting for him. He'd never met a woman quite like her before—so happy, so carefree. He'd never met a woman who excited him quite so much. She was so alive, her body so rich. A shiver of anticipation ran through him. Now, at long last, they would be together. They would make love. And it would be love, not sex. Now he was certain—he loved her.

He unlocked their door and paused as it clicked closed behind him. Jane's dress was hanging neatly over a chair, and there was the frill of black lace underwear there as well. The room was in half-darkness for she had switched off all the lights but for the two at the head of the bed. He could see the long streams of golden hair spread over the pillow.

He walked to the side of the bed, bent over and kissed her gently on the cheek. She made no sign. Her eyes were closed. He could just hear her deep breathing, see the gentle rise and fall of the sheet over her breast.

Stepping back, he took off his own clothes and stood, naked, by her. Dimly, in the long mirror across the room, he could see the dark image of himself, ghost-like. He could even see…

He kissed her again on the cheek. It was such an effort not to kiss her on the lips, not to slide his hands under the sheet to caress those breasts, not to move in beside her and pull her warm body to his. He was tempted—oh, how he was tempted. But she was asleep. Firmly, soundly, absolutely asleep.

There was a funny side to it, he supposed. But he couldn't see it. For minutes he stood there looking at her, looking at that face, showing the innocence of sleep. Then he sighed.

He walked to the other side of the bed and gently eased himself in next to her. She didn't move. He flicked off the lights, then lay there in the darkness, unable to sleep.

Next morning Jane vaguely heard knocking, then a voice whispered for her to go back to sleep. She did. And an hour after that, when she was gently shaken awake, there was the wonderful aroma of coffee close by. She opened her eyes and looked drowsily round the bedroom. 'It's morning,' she said.

'Drink your coffee.' Still half-asleep, she took it, but after the first invigorating mouthful she became fully awake. She looked round again. David was dressed, his bags packed in the middle of the floor. He was smiling at her—rather gloomily, she thought.

'In twenty minutes the bus will be outside to take us to the airport, so you've got fifteen minutes to pack. I thought you'd rather sleep than have breakfast.'

'Yes, I was tired, but I feel better now and…David! What happened last night?'

'What happened last night? Nothing. You came to bed, and when I came up you were asleep—very. So I waited a bit, then I got into bed. And after about three hours I went to sleep myself.'

'But I…we…we were going to…' She blinked at him and said demurely, 'And I was so looking forward to it.'

In a strangled voice he said, 'So was I.'

That was it. She couldn't stop herself laughing. And after a while he, too, managed to laugh—although rather reluctantly.

'No time now,' she said, opening her arms. 'Come and kiss me and then I'll get up and pack. And remember the end of that film? Tomorrow is another day.'

'At the moment I'm still sad about last night. Come on. You've got to pack.' But he did kiss her.

There were more goodbyes. Jean-Claude insisted that they promise to come back. For a start, there were people in Vallere who would want to thank them.

'We'll be back,' she said. 'I haven't been skiing yet.'

The trip to the airport on the bus was uneventful except for the crossing of the new bridge, freshly constructed by the French army. She eyed the apparently rickety structure and said, 'I'm going to close my eyes.' David didn't reply. He was asleep. In fact, he slept all the way, and after a while she dozed off herself.

He was restless in the aeroplane. She thought at first that he was still tired, but he said that wasn't it. 'Was it last night, then? Or are you upset because you didn't go skiing?'

'Not last night. You looked so sweet asleep that I just couldn't have woken you. And if I missed my skiing, you missed your chance to wear your new scarlet outfit.'

'There'll be another chance, I hope. You're going to take me again, aren't you?'

'Possibly. I certainly hope so.'

This answer upset her. 'What d'you mean—possibly? Come on, you've got something to tell me.'

He sighed. 'I have. I've got a confession to make. Jane, I deceived you. I didn't win a holiday. I knew you wouldn't accept me paying for you to come away with me so I made the story up.'

She was silent for a moment and then said, 'I don't like being deceived. D'you want to tell me about any other lies you've told me in the past?'

'There are none.'

'Well, that's a relief. Unless you're lying about that, too. You see, David, now you can't be trusted. You did all this just to get me into bed? It was quite an expense. Are you sure I would have been worth it?'

'Don't say that! You know I—'

'It must have been terrible for you, having to pay for it at long last. Perhaps you're slipping, no longer able to rely on simple good looks. And you didn't get what you wanted. Perhaps I should pay for my share of the holiday.'

'Jane!' She had never seen him so angry. He reached across to her, and grabbed her arms so hard that they hurt. 'I didn't like lying to you! I just wanted us away together where we could—'

'Please, let go of me,' she said coldly. When he had released her she went on, 'So why tell me now?'

'Because I wanted everything between us to be honest. I should have known what you were like, but the past six days have proved it to me. You're the most wonderful person I've ever met. I wanted some time alone with you so we could get to know each other.'

'We *have* got to know each other. And I don't like what I've found out. I told you before—this is a question of trust. You lied to me, and I can't ever trust you again. What we had is over.'

There was a long silence. Then he said, 'I deserve all that so I won't argue. But I desperately hope that it's not true. Believe it or not, Jane, I do love you.'

She stared out of the window and didn't reply.

After half an hour she sighed and reached for his hand. 'We've got to stay friends,' she said. 'For a start, it's the only way I'll ever get to wear that scarlet suit. But don't think I've forgiven you. And take warning. One day I'll go behind your back.'

CHAPTER TEN

THE stewardess smiled down at them both. 'Dr Kershaw and Miss Cabot? I didn't realise we had famous people on board, or I'd have brought you some champagne. There's a message from the hospital. A Mr Moreton wants to have a word with you before the conference he's arranged.'

Jane looked up at the girl blankly. 'Who's famous? And who's Mr Moreton? And what conference?'

Beside her David groaned softly. 'I think I can guess,' he said. Then he looked up at the stewardess and said, 'We've changed our minds. Could we have a couple of brandies, please?'

When they were holding the drinks he said, 'Vallere was in the news all over Europe. The British papers will have got hold of it and our names will be known. A doctor and a nurse go for a holiday and spend the week giving medical help after an avalanche. It's a wonderful story.'

'Oh, Lord,' she said. 'And I told people I was going to meet relatives in Yorkshire. I've been caught lying. I'll be in the same trouble as Megan.'

'Not quite. You're a heroine. There'll be no awkward questions.'

'Except what I was doing away with you. I don't want to meet anyone, David. Let's just creep out of the back. And who's this Moreton fellow, anyway?'

'I've met him, he's a sound man. He's in charge of public relations for the hospital. He did quite a good job of sorting out that problem with Megan Taylor and Charles Grant-Liffley. I think we should do what he wants.'

'But he wants us to talk to reporters,' she said wildly. 'Presumably have our photographs taken and so on.'

'If we meet them and give them what they want, they won't bother us any more. It should be a pleasant meeting, Jane. They don't want to harass you as they did Megan.'

'I just don't like reporters. But I'll do as you say. And I don't like being called a heroine when all I did was act as a nurse.'

He hugged her comfortingly. 'Drink your brandy,' he said. 'It'll make you feel better.'

Somehow Mr Moreton managed to meet them straight off the plane. Jane quite took to him. He was a short, round man with a perpetually hopeful expression. 'Quite frankly, the hospital could do with a bit of good publicity,' he said. 'That Grant-Liffley business did us no good at all. It's not for me to tell you what to say, but if you could drop the name of the hospital into an answer, I'd be happy.'

'I'm not very keen on saying anything,' Jane said.

Mr Moreton looked as if he'd been slapped. 'Please,' he said. 'Honestly, it'll save so much trouble.'

'All right,' she said grumpily, 'but David will have to do most of the talking. Now I'm just going into that Ladies to see what I look like.'

A few minutes later, they followed Mr Moreton into a room where two chairs had been placed on a little platform. There was a bewildering array of microphones on a table and, as soon as they entered, the popping of flash bulbs. There were even two television cameras. I'm not going to enjoy this, she thought.

*　　*　　*

Mr Moreton offered them a lift home, but Jane had her car in the car park and in turn she offered to drive David home. There didn't seem much point in trying to keeping their affair a secret any more—they had just announced it to the world.

'I thought that went very well,' Mr Moreton said. 'I'll report to the CEO. He'll be pleased. Will you drop in to see him tomorrow? I'll know he'll want to see you.'

'It'll be a pleasure,' she said shortly. She got into her car and reached over to open the passenger door for David. Somehow Mr Moreton had arranged to have the car brought to the front of the airport.

David was silent until they were on the M56. Then he said cautiously, 'That wasn't too bad, was it? The reporters seemed quite a pleasant lot, and the questions they asked were fair.'

It was a while before she replied. 'I know the situation is different now,' she said. 'But you referred to me as your fiancée. That means we're supposed to be engaged. Engaged to be married. You're supposed to ask me. I'm supposed to agree. It was a good thing my hands were hidden or they might have noticed I wasn't wearing a ring.'

'Did what I said upset you?'

'Yes, it did. It leaves me with an awful lot of explaining to do to friends and family. I'll have to get disengaged.'

'Sorry. But I just thought that respectable theatre nurses and doctors didn't sleep together until they were at least engaged.'

'It's not funny! I've got to live through this. You're the man, it's all right for you. I never wanted to be on the front page of half the newspapers in the country.'

'Fair enough. But I'll bet you take a good picture.'

His voice became more serious. 'But there's something you should remember—that both of us should remember. Without us more than a few people would have suffered far more than they did. Three or four would have died. You know that, don't you? And I'll bet there's one baby that's going to be called Jeanne because of you. Aren't you glad you did it? Aren't you glad you were able to do it?'

'Yes,' she said flatly, 'I'm glad.' After a pause she went on, 'I wonder if I need a change from being a scrub nurse? Perhaps I need something new in my life. I could retrain and become one of these disaster nurses. It would be interesting work. And I'd go all over the world.'

Now it was his turn to speak flatly. 'Yes. But remember you're an excellent theatre nurse.'

She drove to his flat, and walked round to the back of the car as he took out his luggage. 'We're still on holiday,' he said, 'till breakfast time on Monday. Why not stay and spend the last few hours of it with me?'

As she looked at him, Jane suddenly realised several things. Because of her conversation with Ann Deeds, she'd made assumptions about David that hadn't been true, that he'd been a casual love 'em and leave 'em type. *She'd* been the one to stress that what they'd had had been a casual affair, not David. She knew now that David was very well aware of the impact his looks had on women, and after his treatment at the hands of Diane he'd been right to be wary.

But he wasn't that young doctor any more. He was a grown man who'd suffered and had had to change his career plans, which must have hurt a lot. Because of that he knew what he wanted now, and he'd continued to insist that he loved her—*her*—Jane Cabot, not countless other women. She suddenly understood that David's announcement of their engagement at the airport stemmed from two reasons—one, that he genuinely loved her and, two, that he wanted, because of that love, to protect her as best he could from any uncomfortable comments in the press.

She grew warm with pleasure as she also understood something which should have been blindingly obvious. Although he hadn't been able to propose conventionally, she was pretty sure that he'd wanted to, and probably soon would if she gave him a chance to. She couldn't continue to be angry with him when his motivates had been so wonderful. Abruptly realising how the silence had stretched as David had waited for an answer, she said, 'All right.' Then she lifted out her own bags. Any serious talk could come later. Now they needed to recover from their stress and tiredness.

It was late afternoon, just getting dark. David had arranged to leave the heating on so the flat was warm. While Jane phoned her house-mates to tell them not to expect her, he rattled round in the kitchen.

'A scratch meal,' he told her. 'I could phone out for a take-away, but this will do us.' There was cheese on crispbread, tinned soup and a couple of instant meals out of the freezer. It felt like a picnic. And there was the usual bottle of wine.

'Not exactly the meal we had last night,' he said, 'but the company is just as good.'

'You don't miss Jean-Claude, then?'

Afterwards, they dragged the couch to where they could look out over the river, and sat side by side. She yawned. They were both still short of sleep. 'Bath and bed, I think,' she said. 'May I stay the night?'

'Of course. You're always welcome,' he said, equally urbanely. 'D'you think I should have the first bath? Then you might have to decide whether to wake me.'

She pondered. 'There's an answer to that problem. It's a big bath, we could get in together.'

He reached over and unbuttoned her shirt. 'What a good idea. I'll help you get undressed.'

There wasn't all that much room in the bath, and he suggested that she get in with her back to him. That was nice. His legs wrapped themselves round her, squeezing her hips. His hands were…well, his hands were everywhere. He washed her back, ran rivulets of soapy water down her breasts, rinsed them off with his hands. He took her by the shoulders and made her lean back against his thighs, hard abdomen and chest. 'What's that?' she asked, and turned even pinker when he didn't answer.

Eventually she climbed out and reached for a towel. 'I haven't been so thoroughly washed since my mother did me,' she told him. 'Now, you stay in there a few minutes more and wash yourself. And this night I promise not to go to sleep.'

She padded through to the bedroom and took a thin white nightdress out of her bag. She hadn't worn it yet. It had been a new one, bought for him. She slid into the freshly made bed and waited.

How did she feel? Nervous? Yes. But there was a feeling of inevitability about this, and she knew she'd been waiting for it for a long time.

He walked into the bedroom. Once again there were only the bedside lights on and his body was silhouetted against the doorway. He was clothed solely in a towel. He let it drop. She had a quick sight of his aroused body, and then he was in bed with her.

She reached for him. This was something they would do together. First they kissed, a hard violent kiss, pressing their bodies together as if every possible inch of skin needed to be in contact with the other's. Her hands clutched at his back and neck as she opened her lips to him so his tongue could taste all of her. She was warm, warm, and she could feel his body heat matching hers. Their breathing was heavy, and she could feel his heart thumping against her. Then he placed his hands on her shoulders and eased her away. 'No hurry,' he said.

He made her lie on her back, told her to put her hands behind her head, to relax. Then he started to kiss her again. But this time each kiss was feather-light, over her forehead, down each cheek, the tip of her chin. Then he eased back the covers and his head roamed over the rest of her body. It was both calming and exciting. She giggled. She'd never felt like this before. Calming and exciting. That was impossible. But it was happening.

Then, slowly, it wasn't calming any more. She reached down to clutch his shoulders, grasping the muscles there, her legs tensing and moving with desire. It was so good! Now she wanted him—she wanted to give as well as take. She took his arms and pulled him so that he was lying on top of her. 'David,' she gasped, 'I want you, I want you.'

'And I want you, darling.' His voice was hoarse with desire. He kissed her, a deep, deep kiss, and then she held his hips and urged him into her. 'Ah,' she sighed, 'that is so good.'

But that was merely the start. He moved in her, with her, her body knowing what his wanted. There would be no stopping now. 'David,' she screamed. 'David, David, David.' Her body arched as she heard his urgent cry, and together they reached ecstasy.

He lay across her, damp body on damp body. She could feel his heart beating, though not so fast as before. 'I love you, Jane,' he murmured. Then he fell asleep.

Jane woke early, clear-headed and happy. David was still asleep so she tiptoed out of the bedroom, picking up her discarded nightdress as she did so. She would go back to bed and take him some tea. In the kitchen she looked through the largely empty drawers until she found what she wanted—a kitchen knife, razor sharp. Then she made the tea.

He was awake when she returned to the bedroom, and he first saw the two mugs. 'I should have done that,' he complained mildly. 'What are you doing with my best kitchen knife?' His voice was curious, not alarmed.

She put the mugs by the bed, and turned to the chair where he'd left his trousers the night before. 'I'm feeling symbolic,' she said.

He watched in amazement as she pulled the thick leather belt free from the trouser loops. Then she took the knife and carefully cut a notch in the belt. 'You've slept with me at last,' she said. 'I'm one of your conquests. Isn't that what men do—cut notches in their belts?'

His grim expression made her a little apprehensive. Stark naked, he climbed out of bed, came over and took the knife from her. 'All right, it's what men do,' he said. He walked to the other chair, where she had unceremoniously dumped her own clothes. There were her blue jeans, held up by a similar belt. Carefully, he cut through the belt.

'What are you doing?' She supposed it was fair. She'd cut his belt so he'd cut hers.

'I'm being symbolic, too. You're not one of my conquests, I'm one of yours. I told you, but you never listened. I love you. I've loved you for weeks. I've tried to show it, but all you've done is shout "casual" at me. Jane, there's nothing casual about my feelings for you. I love you. Will you marry me?'

She could make a joke of it all. It would serve him right—perhaps. But she wasn't going to. 'Of course I'll marry you,' she said. 'David, there's no one in the whole wide world who could make me as happy as you do.'

He strode to her, pulled her to him and kissed her. 'We're going to stay together—for ever?' he asked.

'For ever, my darling.'

EPILOGUE

'WE HAD hoped to keep our engagement a secret for a while,' Jane told Sue and Megan.

'Announcing it on television and in all the papers is a funny way of keeping it a secret,' Sue said. 'But congratulations anyway.'

'Where's the ring?' Megan asked.

'We're going shopping on Saturday. And we've already decided on a honeymoon. We're going back skiing.'

'Some people are gluttons for punishment.'

She moved in with David—it seemed pointless not to do so. He bought her a glorious jade ring, jade because it sounded similar to Jane. And they planned their wedding for the following winter so that they could go back to the same hotel, meet Jean-Claude again and she could wear her scarlet skiing outfit. And each night they sat together, looking over the river.

It was three months later, and the end of the day's work. Jane had come home early. She heard David come in, and hid a letter under the cushion. 'Tea's here,' she called. 'Come and sit with me.'

He sat with her, kissed her and reached for his tea.

She hoped this would go well. 'I'm remembering,' she said. 'On the plane, when you told me how you hadn't won the skiing holiday at all. I said you'd gone behind my back. And one day I'd do the same to you.'

'You're very welcome to,' he said amiably. 'Anything you want to do, I want to do, too.'

'Well, I have done. Sort of. You know I told you I was engaged for a while? You don't mind I lived with another man?'

'I lived with women,' he pointed out. 'I'm not going to object. I just think this John…Gilmore was a fool to give someone like you up.'

'There was a big future for him in Boston. He's working with a top man there.' She took a deep breath. 'I wrote to him, David.'

That did surprise him. But he wasn't upset. 'I'm sure you had a good reason,' he said calmly. 'D'you want him to come to our wedding?'

'No. Or perhaps yes. But mostly I think I want you to go to see him. I copied your case notes, David, and sent them out to him. His boss is doing wonderful work on restoring nerves—he's the man who sews hands back on. They've looked at your case notes. They think there's a chance they could restore the full feeling and articulation in your hand, David. You could still be a surgeon.'

The silence stretched on immeasurably. 'You… did…that for me?'

'I thought it would it make you happier. Yes, I did it for you.'

He kissed her, then grinned. 'We'll invite them both to our wedding,' he said.

Watch out next month for Megan's story in the final part of Gill Sanderson's vibrant trilogy.

MILLS & BOON®

Makes any time special™

Mills & Boon publish 29 new titles every month. Select from...

Modern Romance™   Tender Romance™

Sensual Romance™

Medical Romance™   Historical Romance™

MAT2

For better, for worse... for ever

Brides and Grooms

FREE

4 BOOKS
AND A SURPRISE GIFT!

We would like to take this opportunity to thank you for reading this Mills & Boon® book by offering you the chance to take FOUR more specially selected titles from the Medical Romance™ series absolutely FREE! We're also making this offer to introduce you to the benefits of the Reader Service™—

- ★ FREE home delivery
- ★ FREE monthly Newsletter
- ★ FREE gifts and competitions
- ★ Exclusive Reader Service discounts
- ★ Books available before they're in the shops

Accepting these FREE books and gift places you under no obligation to buy; you may cancel at any time, even after receiving your free shipment. Simply complete your details below and return the entire page to the address below. *You don't even need a stamp!*

YES! Please send me 4 free Medical Romance books and a surprise gift. I understand that unless you hear from me, I will receive 6 superb new titles every month for just £2.40 each, postage and packing free. I am under no obligation to purchase any books and may cancel my subscription at any time. The free books and gift will be mine to keep in any case.

M0ZEC

Ms/Mrs/Miss/Mr ....Initials ....
BLOCK CAPITALS PLEASE

Surname ....

Address ....

....

....Postcode ....

Send this whole page to:
UK: FREEPOST CN81, Croydon, CR9 3WZ
EIRE: PO Box 4546, Kilcock, County Kildare (stamp required)

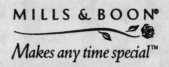